I0657127

Murder In Key West 5

Murder and Mayhem In Paradise

Murder In Key West 5

Murder and Mayhem
In Paradise

Edited by Shirrel Rhoades

ABSOLUTELY AMAZING eBOOKS

Published by Whiz Bang LLC, 926 Truman Avenue, Key West, Florida 33040, USA.

Murder In Key West 5 copyright © 2018 by Gee Whiz Entertainment LLC. Electronic compilation/ paperback edition copyright © 2018 by Whiz Bang LLC.

All rights reserved. No part of this book may be reproduced, scanned, or transmitted in any form or by any means, electronic or mechanical, including photocopying, recording, or any information storage and retrieval system, without permission in writing from the publisher. Please do not participate in or encourage piracy of copyrighted materials in violation of the author's rights. Purchase only authorized ebook editions.

This is a work of fiction. Names, characters, places, and incidents either are the product of the author's imagination or are used fictitiously, and any resemblance to actual persons, living or dead, businesses, companies, events, or locales is entirely coincidental. While the author has made every effort to provide accurate information at the time of publication, neither the publisher nor the author assumes any responsibility for errors, or for changes that occur after publication. Further, the publisher does not have any control over and does not assume any responsibility for author or third-party websites or their contents. How the ebook displays on a given reader is beyond the publisher's control.

For information contact:
Publisher@AbsolutelyAmazingEbooks.com

ISBN-13: 978-1945772856 (Absolutely Amazing Ebooks)
ISBN-10: 1945772859

Believe it or not, here is another volume of *Murder In Key West* – the fifth in the series. As usual, its publication coincides with the fifth annual Mystery Fest Key West, a gathering of famous mystery writers, aspiring writers, and die-hard mystery fans.

This book is dedicated to them.

Murder In Key West 5

Murder and Mayhem In Paradise

Murder In Key West 5

INTRODUCTION TO MURDER

Key West – its original name was *Cayo Hueso*. The Spanish words mean "Island of Bones." That epithet seems appropriate, considering the nature of the stories in this book, ten tales of "Murder and Mayhem in Paradise."

This 4-square-mile island located at the tail-end of the Florida peninsula has been the site of many murders throughout its history.

Warring tribes of indigenous natives piled the island with bones of the dead. 17th-century pirates left a few dead bodies behind. Salvagers made fortunes off wrecking ships, many passengers drowning in the process. During the Cuban Missile Crisis the island was crawling with CIA and other black ops types. Gerry Patrick Hemming trained paramilitary troops on nearby No Name Key. Later, drug smugglers ran rampant in the Florida Straights. During the '80s drug dealers dropped off Burger King bags filled with cash at Key West's City Hall. About then, the FBI called the Key West Police Department "a continuing criminal enterprise." Even today, dead bodies turn up now and again. Violent crime in Key West is about double the national average.

Ernest Hemingway made his home in Key West during the '30s. Death and violence were constant themes in his life and writing.

Another literary resident, Tennessee Williams wrote of "murder, cannibalism, castration, madness, incest, rape, adultery, nymphomania and homosexuality."

Over the years mystery writers have crowded the island, ink-smudged personages ranging from Larry Shames and John Leslie to Tom Corcoran and Stuart Woods.

So we're happy to carry on the tradition of murder in Key West with this anthology series. Fictional murders, that is.

But read it with your back to the wall.

- Shirrel Rhoades
Key West

1

All that Glitters

Jack Mazur

had some gold, sure. Everyone down here has
some kind of alternate savings plan. I had two
pounds! You don't sneeze at that. Where it came from
is no one's business but where it went is everyone's.

My financial advisers, in New York, had always
told me to invest in gold. Its depletion in the market
was always minimal. Beat the hell out of the
dollar! Unfortunately I insisted after one visit to bring
a pound home with me. Why? To show off that's
why. There were only a half dozen people I would show
this to. Thought that I trusted them all. But, in the
end, I was a show off!

Recently I had been spending some time in an
effort to run for mayor of Key West. Crusty and as
unpolished as I am I knew I could win this thing. My
opposition began to fall like Key West limes during

harvest time. Nice to be loved. But I was a jerk, had a record and was well known for public drunkenness. I've eaten more bologna sandwiches than a preteen in junior high school. Thanks to the county!

One day I get home and inspect my one-pound of gold molded into a heavy bar. But it ain't there. Man, it ain't there! I had several hours of fidgety activity. I call Jack and I call Max who happens to be staying in the Best Western on South Street. Max has credentials through several "black" agencies in the U.S. government. He's a spook. Jack just continuously tells me to take it easy. I do my best. After we all get together we decide in unison that this is the work of Smut! Wasn't easy. We had a lot of arguments. No matter how you handled Smut he kept coming back. I never saw my gold again but I did hear of Smut's demise.

~ ~ ~

The whaleboat, not the speedboat usually used, drifted with the current toward a bridge in the upper Keys. There was a transaction to be handled and money to be made. There was nothing legal about it. It was dark but there were tinges of light far off to the east.

Every transaction brought a jolt of nervous energy to Freddie Garcia recently paroled from the Big Pine work prison. Convicted and paroled for the very reason he was afloat this very minute. Life lessons are important to individuals but so is making money. It is exceptionally quiet except for the occasional beer truck headed to Key West and Duval Street. Under the bridge Freddie sees some movement where he didn't expect it.

He tied off to a mangrove branch and adjusted his eyes. Then what his eyes saw dropped his heart and his ability to contemplate reality. The scene involved what looked like an older naked man and obviously a young child. Freddie wasn't carrying any guns on this night. But he was carrying a half a dozen Viet Nam-era hand grenades. In a fast reflex of emotion, thought and rationality he pulled the pin on two and tossed them into the water where the cement met the on coming tide. The explosions were tremendous on this quiet night. The sick psycho and the young child screamed and ran off in different directions. One waddling with a horrible limp. Freddie pulled out his cell phone and called 911. He explained what he had seen and what he had done. His drug store bought phone was untraceable but he knew that the sheriff would know that only one local guy had the audacity to go boating, if that's what one would call it, with hand grenades. There would be no square grouper today. Freddie split the scene at a low speed as to not draw any more attention.

The next day Freddie visited Joe Beans on Watson Street in Key West. They were old friends. He explained to Joe what he had seen and what he would like to be done. Joe concurred with violent anger throwing his coffee cup through the plate glass sliding door. It had become apparent to both who the sicko was. With the greasy long hair and the unmistakable limp only one name came to mind. But then another name came to the fore. Within minutes Joe had Max on the line. In a few more minutes a decision had been made.

Several days later Max and Joe were having beers

at the Parrot. Their discussion was in low tones and away from the bar. It didn't last long. Max, per his habit, disappeared.

Later that day Freddie and Joe went fishing in the same whaleboat on the Atlantic side of Lower Sugarloaf. They had a few beers and caught a few fish but their hearts weren't in it. Anger washed over them like storm waves. They motored into the local mangroves and tied up in a hidden channel and hiked into a secret campsite once inhabited by a World War Two U-boat captain. There they downed their anger and their angst with alcoholic chasers. There was only one solution. There was only one way. There was only God to answer to.

The anger was shared by Max. This was one crime he could not adjust to. No way. For several days he searched under bridges from Boca Chica to Islamorada. He found a lot of bums and he saw a lot of Key Weirdness but he didn't find Smut. Not right away. But he kept at it. He was not recognizable in his long hair hippie wig, cut-off jeans and dirty T-shirt. After several days he found his prey in a dive bar in Marathon. He didn't act but just observed. Then he followed. He found the new bridge habitat of the molester and when Smut was away he searched through his few belongings. Old rags, empty beer cans and child porn in foreign magazines! Max had dispensed with two dictators in the Banana Republics. Never batted an eyelash. Now he puked all over the rags. He left the scene, changed his disguise, and got himself a nice room in a good hotel. He watched the Republican presidential debates on television. It was laughable. But his prey was not. He made his plan.

Max was not a religious man but on this day he got down on his knees next to his hotel bed and begged Jesus for mercy for the crime he was about to commit. He wasn't sure it was necessary.

The next night Smut staggered and limped to his home under a bridge not far from Marathon. He noticed a stronger stench than usual from amongst his few belongings. He tossed these items into the channel below where it happened a few bull sharks were hunting. Then he opened his magazines.

Another magazine was opened a few yards away but it was of a different type. A clip of ammunition was inserted.

On Watson Street Joe remembered his friend Jack talking about his short-lived job at the local psychiatric center. He had talked about this guy Smut, who when out of money and hungry, entered the establishment and claimed he was suicidal. According to Florida law he had to be observed for five days. He got fed, got a bed, showered, got new clothes, lived in air-conditioned comfort and told Jack to change the channel on the television continuously. Then he was discharged with a small prescription of psychotropics that he sold on the street for a pint of vodka. Over and over again! Old Smut was well known. The psychiatric hospital was a hotel to him. And free! Thank you dumbass taxpayers! Joe did not sleep well that night.

Well after dark Max showed himself under the bridge. "Hello Smut." The pervert looked up from his magazine with his pants around his ankles. "Get the fuck outta here, this is my home!"

"Sorry, bud. But you went over the line."

"Hey, you're the guy what shot me!" Then he threw a hidden knife at Max, which was easily ducked. Max shot him in the carotid. The yelping was loud and long. As he began to pull the trigger again he heard, "Drop it!" To Max' right stood the newly elected sheriff in his pressed green uniform with a gun pointed directly at him. They knew each other. Max did as he was told.

The sheriff raised his pistol and put three holes in Smut's head. The child molester was dead. The blood from the carotid shot had dripped into the channel and shark fins could be seen right at the water's edge. Neither the sheriff nor Max spoke. As if on cue they picked up the body and tossed it into the channel. Happy sharks did what sharks do.

"Now, beat it," said the sheriff." There was no need for conversation. By the dawn Max was back in Panama.

In Key West Joe awoke with a jolt just as the first bullet hit Smut. He got up and made a pot of coffee then went out on the porch to watch the sun come up. He, too, prayed to Jesus. Then the trash trucks came.

~ ~ ~

It was some weeks later when a scientist from Mote Marine Laboratories was doing research on the digestive system of Bull sharks that a remarkable discovery was made. After catching a very large shark the scientist involved eviscerated the creature and found some surprising items. This was off the wrecks on the coral reef. Inside the stomach of this shark the scientist found a Barbie doll, a copy of the King James bible, about a hundred fish hooks, and there amongst the bile and other fish digestive oils, things that looked like human remains and a one pound block of gold! Some days fishing are better than others.

2

Four Fingers and the Bomber

Shirrel Rhoades

Wharton "Four Fingers" Dalessandro was enjoying a Red Stripe at Schooner Wharf when his pal Dunk Reid sat down on a stool beside him. The two men played chess most days on the boardwalk outside the bar, but today was Time Out, this being the final day of the 36th Conch Republic Independence Celebration.

The Conch Republic was born back in 1982 when locals "seceded" from the United States, then immediately surrendered and asked for "war reparations."

Fat chance of that. But the fanciful concept did catch people's imaginations.

The Conch Republic became an alternate name for Key West, flying its own blue flag, issuing ersatz passports, and claiming its own one-boat navy. Each year there's a weeklong festival (well, actually ten days). From a musical reenactment to a parade to a conch fritter eating contest to bed races to a pirate's ball, the carryings-on stretch from Friday till the following Sunday.

Today was the Conch Republic Diplomats Brunch, a gathering at the Hog's Breath Saloon on Front Street. Dunk Reid was supposed to be there, leading a drinks-held-high toast to the island's faux independence.

But here was Dunk on the next stool.

"What's up, ol' pal?" said Four Fingers. He downed the Red Stripe and turned to examine his friend.

"Stump's dead," he replied. His lips quivered as he spilled out the words.

Rathbone "Stump" Bethel was a city commissioner. He represented a portion of Bahama Village, the area in Key West that had once been called Nigger Town. A 16-block area southwest of Whitehead Street, it had been populated by immigrants from the Bahamas. Today it's much more gentrified, featuring a number of popular restaurants.

"What happened to him? Heart attack?" Stump's cardiovascular problems had been an issue during the last election, but he'd heartily won his seat on the city commission.

"Not his ticker. A ticking time bomb. Somebody blew up his car, him in it."

"Police have any clues?"

"Not that I know of. I'm surprised Chief Johnny Leigh hasn't called you."

Four Fingers was a former NYPD Homicide Detective. Having retired to Key West, he worked as a housepainter to supplement his pension. The Police Chief sometimes called on his services. He had a knack for solving crimes after only a few minutes of careful observation.

"Haven't had a jingle," he said, holding up his iPhone.

"Lemme see that," grumbled Dunk Reid, grabbing the device out of his friend's hand. "Just as I figured. You've let your battery run down again. It's dead as an iguana trying to cross US1."

Four Fingers had a bad habit of forgetting to charge his phone. Johnny Leigh might have tried to call him about the commissioner's murder. He wouldn't have known.

"Yeah, well." Four Fingers was stewing. Maybe he could make up for his oversight by putting his mind to the death of Stump Bethel. He shifted his mind into crime scene mode. "Tell me more about the murder."

Dunk squinted his eyes, concentrating. "Like I said, it was a car bombing. Chief Leigh said it was some kind of pipe bomb, based on the fragments in the wreckage."

"Did Stump have any known enemies?"

"Politicians always have enemies. But he won last fall's election by an overwhelming majority. People in Bahama Village liked him. He was their hope for the future."

"Has he always been a politician?"

"Pretty much," said Dunk. "He's been everything from chicken catcher to head of Mosquito Control.

That's how he got his nickname, stumping for one elected position or another."

"Married?"

"Forty years. Just celebrated their anniversary. His wife adored him."

"Could she build a pipe bomb?"

The bartender deposited a Red Stripe in front of Four Fingers, with another for the little man. Dunk took a sip, then said, "Not likely. Bessie was unmechanical. Barely knew how to operate a pencil sharpener."

Four Fingers gave a little grunt of disappointment. "That eliminates the most likely suspect. Always look at the spouse first."

"Then who?"

"Did Stump play around?" he said by way of answer.

"Doubt it. His wife used to joke about his ED, same affliction as Bob Dole. At their age it wasn't a big deal. Both in their late 60s."

"Gamble?"

"Once a week he played five card stud, five cents a hand. Him and the mayor and a couple other movers-and-shakers. Nothing big."

"Any large debts?"

"Don't think so. He owned several rental properties outright. That rental income, his commission salary, and Social Security gave him a pretty comfortable life. He and Bessie weren't extravagant people."

"Any personal grudges? Feud with a neighbor? Maybe a dispute over a property line?" Housing plots in Key West were always being challenged. If you surveyed from one end of the block you got a different answer from a survey started at the other.

"Not that I know of."

"How 'bout trouble with a relative? Problems with a bad renter? Or a run-in with a local drug dealer?" Bahama Village was a drive-thru depot for weed, opioids, and other illegal concoctions.

"No, no, and no. Told you, most everybody liked 'im."

"Somebody didn't."

"Got a point there," Dunk admitted. "He's dead enough."

Four Fingers took another sip of his beer. "Who did he run against for that city commission position?"

"Mighty Mike Powell. It was a fairly contentious campaign between the two. Mike made all kinda unfounded aspersions. Accused Stump of embezzling city funds. But everybody knew that wasn't true. Probably cost Mike the election. People on this island don't like candidates badmouthing each other."

"Mike Powell? Doesn't he own a hole-in-the-wall garage on Thomas Street? Mighty Mike's Motors, I think it's called."

"Yep, that's him."

"Does he do much business in that outta-the-way location?" Deep in Bahama Village, Thomas Street was off the main thoroughfares.

"Not many customers. Probably why he was running for office. To supplement his income."

"Anything noteworthy about his garage?"

"Naw. He specializes in Jeeps, but there ain't that many of them hereabout."

"Why Jeeps?"

"Knows 'em inside and out. He worked in the motor pool when he was in Desert Storm."

"He served in Kuwait and Iraq?"

"Came out a master sergeant. Used to joke that he still had desert sand in his boots."

"A guy who served in Desert Storm might've learned how to make an IED."

"A what?"

"An Improvised Explosive Device. That's a homemade bomb them ragheads use to blow up Jeeps and Humvees and other military vehicles."

"You don't think −?"

"A contentious election makes for hard feelings. A hotheaded ex-soldier who knows auto mechanics and amateur bomb-making sounds like an awfully good suspect."

Dunk was looking past Four Finger's shoulder. His eyes widened and his Adam's apple bobbed. "Don't look now, but there's Mighty Mike Powell coming in the entrance next to the bandstand."

Four Fingers casually shifted his position, catching sight of a burly redheaded man wearing a threadbare T-shirt and grease-stained blue jeans. The T-shirt was emblazoned with the word PARROTHEAD. Hmm, a Jimmy Buffett fan.

"Hey, Mike," the retired homicide detective called to the new arrival. "Lemme buy you a drink."

Mighty Mike Powell sidled over. "Do I know you?"

"This is Four Fingers Dalessandro," Dunk spoke up. "Him and me play chess t'gether."

"Hello, Dunk," nodded the carrot-top man. "You still playing that sissy game?"

"Hey, I was the high school champ. Don't you remember? You were only a year or two behind of me."

But Mighty Mike was no longer interested. He looked Dunk's companion over. "Why d' they call you Four Fingers?"

The lanky man held up his right hand, displaying the four digits. The index finger was missing.

"How'd you do that?"

"Fishing accident. Fish won."

"Hmm. That sucks."

"I'm used to it."

"Buy you a beer?" Dunk offered. Feeling awkward, considering the conversation he and Four Fingers had been having just before Mighty Mike walked in.

"Why not? Been a helluva a morning."

"Stump, you mean?" offered Dunk Reid.

Mighty Mike frowned. "Never get used to seeing a man turned into hamburger meat," he said.

Four Fingers signaled for another round, pointing to Mike Powell to order an additional beer. "Did you see a lot of that over in Iraq?" he said to the man with the greasy clothing and arms covered in blue tattoos.

"More'n I care to talk about."

"That where you learned to make pipe bombs?"

"Hey, what are you saying −?"

"Just asking."

"You think I blew up that two-bit snake-oil salesman? You can't prove that."

"Sure I can."

"How can you do that? I didn't leave any traces. Wiped my fingerprints off everything." Mighty Mike was not all that bright, as it turned out.

"There you have it," said Four Fingers. "QED."

"Huh?"

"*Quod erat demonstrandom.* Proves my theory. You killed Stump Bethel."

"You dirty bastard –" The big man rose up like a grizzly bear about to attack.

"Hold it right there," came a gruff voice from behind him. Police Chief Johnny Leigh had arrived at Schooner Wharf, accompanied by a couple of tough-looking plainclothes cops.

"What the hell?" Mighty Mike exclaimed, but the two cops grabbed those tattooed arms and slapped cuffs on his wrists.

"You can't do this," he shouted.

"It's done," said Chief Leigh. "You're under arrest for the murder of James Rathbone Bethel. I heard what you said to Dalessandro."

"Screw you. That jerk Stump Bethel got what he deserved. He played dirty in last fall's election."

Chief Johnny Leigh shrugged. "Way I remember it, you were the one making all kinda false claims about Bethel. Voters didn't like that."

Mighty Mike spat on the Schooner Wharf's dirt floor. "I want a lawyer," he demanded.

"Yeah, yeah. You'll have to wait your turn. Might get you a public defender in a day or two."

"Hey, I got my own lawyer – Edward Gluckman. He's got an office opposite the courthouse."

"Good luck on that. Sharp Eddie skipped town last week with his secretary. His wife has filed for divorce."

"That's damn inconsiderate of him – just when I need legal representation."

"Tough break," said the police chief, not meaning it.

Four Fingers turned to Johnny Leigh. "You arrived here just in time. What brings you by Schooner Wharf on a Sunday?"

"Looking for you. Your phone wasn't working."

"Forgot to charge it. What did you want?"

The police chief glanced at the cuffed man. "Nothing now," he said.

The bartender spoke up, "D'you still want that third beer, Four Fingers?"

"Yeah, I'll drink it," he said. "Think I just earned it. Put it on Chief Leigh's tab."

3

Tide Kings

Rick Ollerman

He'd made it to the island first. That was the important thing. It was a lot easier for him to finish things if they were looking for him somewhere else. Of course they'd catch up to him eventually, soon even, but that would be fine. He only wanted them to think he was running away like an animal. He'd lead them a merry chase he would, but Tony D'Amico would never flee in a panic from a bunch of cops.

Once he'd left Miami, he'd driven north and then across Alligator Alley gulfside to Ft. Myers. Tony'd left his car in the long-term lot at the airport and took a shuttle to some random hotel. From there a cab ride to the ferry terminal, a three and a half hour ride back home to Key West, and he was lost to them. For now.

They'd get back on him at some point. Someone would get clever and circle back around when their leads got cold. The important thing was that the car hadn't been registered to him and they knew nothing about that anyway. They were, however, very familiar with his home, his friends, his habits. And his girl.

Tony d'Amico spent the first day on the island lurking about with the tourists, keeping away from his people, getting a few things set the way they'd need to be. He came to appreciate the silly little Key West chickens everywhere. He remembered the days of the feral cats, the little bastards that wouldn't let you get close to an alley or a dumpster or any sort of out of the way corner without sounding like a mass of rabid house pets crossed with Africanized bees.

The island's bounty took care of those vicious creatures and now you had harmless little chickens laying in the grass and under bushes, and walking along the sidewalks during the day. D'Amico found that he liked watching the chickens. For some reason he couldn't get used to seeing them on his Key West, as if one exotic animal had been replaced with a different one. What would come next? Lemurs? Three-toed sloths?

That day Tony showed off his native tan and told made up stories of the Conch Republic and did sleight of hand tricks for the youngsters. No one looked at him twice and he let his picture be taken a dozen times. As twilight approached and tourists and locals alike migrated to the western side of the island to watch the sun sink into the far horizons of the ocean. They spoke of the fabled "green flash" and either planned the night's "Duval crawl" pub adventure or reminisced over the days when every other storefront did not advertise three t-shirts for ten dollars. Whatever they did, D'Amico stayed where he was on the island's opposite beach.

He began picking up litter—yogurt cups, aluminum cans, wax paper—and shoving them into the garbage cans set away from the sand. No one looks twice at a guy picking up garbage from the beach. They're either too embarrassed either for themselves or for others; they knew where the refuse came from. Those same people leaving puddles on the floor in front of the public urinals have dry as desert bathroom floors at home.

When enough people had gone, d'Amico rinsed his hands in the seawater and dried them on his shirt as he made his way up the relatively empty Duval Street. There was still nothing for him to worry about. On an island this small, there was no hiding for the cops. There were too many ways to blend in here, and a few of them involved costumes and outrageous behavior. Paradoxically, you were looked at but not seen, watched but not identified. You were a perverse sort of chicken on the sidewalk, only on a parade float or waving a boa outside a drag bar.

He took a left half a mile up and made his way to the alley behind a small white house with a tiny sixteen square foot yard and wooden steps that lead to a door. Grinning between his unshaven cheeks, he put his hand on the doorknob and turned it slowly.

It was unlocked. So Angie was home then. Good.

As he pushed the door open he could hear her singing, softly and gently, and he was about to call her name when he realized the sounds he was hearing weren't any song lyrics. He stopped. There were other sounds, too. Man sounds.

God damn it, Angie, he thought. He almost moved forward and busted it up. He'd had to do it before but he thought those times were past. He took his hand off the knob and lifted his back foot and then put it down again. He couldn't do it. She could put them on him now if he did and that would ruin everything.

For a brief second he felt like putting his forehead through the doorframe but it passed. Slowly a grin reappeared on his face, though not the same one as before, and he backed out of the house, quietly pulling the door shut.

God damn it, Angie.

He'd worked his way into Phil's place where he was having a beer at the bar when Six-Toe walked in. He glanced at Tony but didn't turn his head and found a spot further down the left from d'Amico. Phil nodded to yet another of his regulars before wiping up a beer spill and working his way over. There was a red band along the bottom of the big screen TV above the bar. Tropical Storm Carter had turned north into the Gulf.

"You drinking tonight, Six-Toe?"

Six-Toe kept his voice down. "Not yet, not yet." He gestured with his head. "How long has he been here?"

Phil the bartender looked over at Tony d'Amico. "Tony? Why don't you go over and ask him?"

Six-Toe shook his head. "Tell him the cops are coming. They're sweeping the joints, top to bottom. I'm only just ahead of them."

"How long till they're here?"

"They're just behind me, like I said."

"Right." Phil started off.

"I want his beer," Six-Toe called.

D'Amico had been watching the conversation but he hadn't been able to hear it. Everybody knew Six-Toe though not everyone cared to share a stool with him. When Phil came over and told him what the man had said, d'Amico laughed. "It's about time," he said. "Here," he told Phil, sliding a twenty across the bar top. "Pay my tab and pour him a couple on me. Just don't tell him where they came from."

"If they're starting from this end of the island they'll be here any minute."

"It's perfect," Tony said, grinning. "But I need to ask you one more thing." He slid a fifty after the twenty. Phil didn't even look at it before making it disappear.

"Name it."

"You're a good man, Phil. Look," and Tony leaned closer, as did the bartender. "You still got that skylight on top of this joint?"

"Aye."

"How about I go up and take a look at it?"

"You coming back?"

"Do I need to?"

Phil pulled a ring of keys from his pocket, palming them to keep them from jangling. "Take these. Go out back to the beer crates...."

"I know the way."

Phil grunted. "I bet you do. Just get these back to me as soon as you can."

D'Amico picked up his beer, finished it, and put the mug back on the bar before wiping his lip. "Soon as they pass, Phil. Soon as they pass. Then I'll stand you one myself." He nodded sideways down the bar. "You better take care of Six-Toe. He's looking like he's screwing up his nerve."

"He's screwed up everything else he's ever been involved with. You good?"

"As gold. Be back in a few."

Turning away from Six-Toe with Phil's keys in his hand, d'Amico moved toward the restrooms in the back and then made a sharper left and unlocked a padlocked hasp that took him out to a small outbuilding where Phil kept his stock of beer. Behind him he heard a whoop of joy from Six-Toe whatever-the-hell-his-last-name-was. No one knew what it was because no one cared. Tony'd had faith that someone would let him know the cops were coming. He'd never have thought it would be Six-Toe but at least he was easily paid.

He couldn't lock the door after him but he knew Phil would take care of that. D'Amico climbed to the top of the small building as quietly as he could, then made the short leap to the shingles of the bar building itself. He kept himself low and picked his way carefully up to the fake crow's nest built at the apex of the bar's roof. Laying down on the side away from Duval Street, d'Amico stretched out next to the grimed over skylight, arms across his chest. There was time for a nap. Quick one, anyway.

Twenty minutes later a handful of ice rained down on and around Tony's body. He jolted awake and then didn't move. A second handful of cubes fell and he saw them plainly as they caught the shards of light and neon from Duval as they rolled and tumbled through the air. On his belly, d'Amico worked his way to the edge of the roof and eased his head over the gutter.

"Phil?"

"They're gone."

"When?"

"Just now."

Tony yawned. "I'll be right down."

Phil nodded and started to turn away.

"Wait," Tony said. He pulled Phil's keys from his pocket and tossed them down. "Undo the back door for me, will ya?"

"Will do."

Tony pushed up into a crouch and made his way off the roof the same way he'd gotten up. Once on the sandy ground, he pushed against the back door and it swung open easily. He took the open padlock hanging from the hasp and locked the door up, making it the same way he'd found it when he'd left.

Back at the bar, he asked Phil for another beer. He saw that Six-Toe had gone.

"Don't you want to get out of here?"

D'Amico laughed. "There's plenty of time. They have the whole town to get through." He nodded to his left where most of the people at the bar were looking up at the television set. "Gilligan get off the island?"

"It's the storm," Phil said.

"What storm?" There hadn't been one when Tony had planned on coming to Key West.

"Just a bed wetter," said Phil. "Tropical Storm."

"No hurricane?"

Phil shook his head. "Naw. It'll weaken now. The eye's already falling apart."

Tony laughed again. "Just a nuisance then." Without the eye the storm wouldn't intensify and would collapse on itself. The tourists might get some clouds and rain. Welcome to Key West, kiddies.

Phil plunked a fresh beer in front of him and then moved off to service his other customers. Tony turned and sipped the brew with his back to the bar. He saw no cops walk past the open walls, no patrol cars, nothing. This was going according to plan, he thought. To them, he might be on the island, he might not. So they'd check. If he was in front of them, he'd have to contend with them all night. As it was, he could follow them down Duval and they'd never be the wiser.

When Phil returned, Tony asked him what the cops had said.

"Only if you'd been around lately. I said I hadn't seen you."

"That it?"

"And that you always drank here when you were on the island."

Tony handed over a fifty. "Phil my friend, you pour a shitty beer but you're a hell of a bartender."

The bill disappeared as fast as the others as Phil said, "Go to hell."

"I will. Just one more thing," Tony said, an edge to his voice. "Where can I find Angie these nights?"

Phil stared back at him. "Go outside and wait for an hour. She'll be by."

"You got anything more specific?"

"What specific? It's Key West, man. Shout her name and she'll be there in ten minutes."

Tony didn't like the tone of Phil's voice but he didn't want to push the man. He certainly couldn't afford a scene. Instead he forced a smile, polished off his beer and clapped Phil on the shoulder. Out on the street he crossed to the south looking east as he went. He could see the patrol car then, parked in front of a hydrant in front of a swimwear shop a block and a half away.

He kept going and went into the bar across the street. Heads turned, a few with recognition on their faces. He called those over and bought two pitchers of beer as they told him about the cops that had been in asking about him. D'Amico drank and made up a story where the good part had come from somebody else. The men laughed as they emptied their own glasses. Then he asked about Angie.

As Tony d'Amico walked among the crowds along Duval Street, watching for signs of the police somewhere blocks ahead of him, he knew part of what they were doing was putting on a show. Key West was the end of the line, the last of the islands—at least the ones connected by road—and if he were here, they wanted him to feel trapped. They'd be watching the docks and the airport, too, and the ferry station, and oh, how they'd love it if he made it easy and tried to take Highway 1 out toward the Upper Keys.

But Tony wasn't trapped. He could leave any time he wanted. He just had something to do first.

He moved down a block and then detoured one over and found the Parrot. The two men were there, just like they were supposed to be. When Tony walked in, the smaller of the pair began to stand before his partner put his hand out and bade him sit.

As Tony walked over, the smaller one said, "The cops are looking all over for you!"

D'Amico laughed. All things considered, he was in a pretty good mood. "They think this is the last stop for me," he said, and laughed again.

The bigger man said, "It is an island."

"Don't think so small." Tony pulled back a chair. "May I sit? I need a beer."

The smaller man looked uncomfortable as the larger one said, "Please."

Tony took a seat and looked over for the bartender or a waitress. "What are you guys drinking?"

"We drank it," the big guy said. "Let's do our business. We have a plane to get to and we don't want this Tropical Storm Carter thing to ruin our plans."

Tony turned his head and found one of the TV sets in the bar, invariably turned to the weather station. The satellite and radar pictures showed a swirling mass of clouds, that was all.

"That thing still a Tropical Storm? It'll be downgraded to a Depression soon. Look at it."

"Let's get on with it."

D'Amico took some money out of his pants pocket and put it on the table in front of the smaller guy. "Sure. Let's get on with it. Soon as this guy gets me a couple of beers."

"Hey, you can—"

"Sit down, Johnny," the larger man said. He looked his partner back into his seat, then at Tony. "This is how you want to do this?"

"I told you I'm thirsty."

The larger man shook his head. "Johnny, go to the bar and get Mr. d'Amico a beer. Please."

Johnny snatched up the money.

"Two beers, Johnny," Tony called.

"Please," said his partner. He looked pained when he said, "Why do you want to be like that?"

"Kid looks like an asshole."

"So what are you, the asshole police? Of course he's an asshole. You try to find young help any time lately? This is what you scrape up when you call the employment agency. Believe me, this kid's not half bad for what we use him for."

"What's the other half?"

Johnny showed up with Tony's beers and put them on the table, not too gently.

"Where's my change?"

"Don't you know? You're a good tipper."

Tony looked at the larger man, who shrugged. He picked up one of the mugs, drained half of it away, then gave a long and drawn out belch in the youngster's direction. "Clean that up, will you?"

"Knock it off, Tony," said the larger man. "What's the story?"

From his left front pocket, d'Amico pulled out the key to a Chevy Impala and tossed it on the table. "Long term parking, Ft. Myers airport. Ticket is in the ashtray. Dark green car with Colorado plates. Money's in the trunk."

The larger man started to speak but Tony cut him off.

"All of the money is in the trunk. I already got paid, remember?"

"How's the heat?"

D'Amico finished the first beer. "It's bound to come so I'd move on it quick. Send this guy. He looks quick."

Johnny looked flustered, as if he'd been insulted but didn't quite know how.

Tony kept looking at him. "Do you have bowling shoes, Johnny?" Tony asked. "You look like the kind of guy who would have his own bowling shoes."

Johnny stood up slowly and looked at the larger man. "Why don't you go outside, check the street for the cops, kid? We're going to leave in just a minute."

Without looking back at d'Amico, the slender Johnny smoothed his shirt and picked his way stiffly through the crowded tables and out into the humid nighttime air.

When he was gone both men laughed. D'Amico drank his second beer and the large man told a few stories of how business had changed in Broward County. When both men were dry, he stood up. Tony rose, the two shook hands with some affection, and the larger man left.

Tony was relieved. If he was pinched now he wouldn't have to try to explain the key. His part of the casino job was now over. At the bar, he watched the never-ending looping images of a barely organized storm, only just hanging on to its center. People never got tired of watching this crap.

The key had been handed off, he was seeing the old gang, and the cops thought they were flushing him to one end of the island. He laughed out loud again. Everything was fine, except for one thing.

He still needed to talk to Angie.

She ended up being two blocks down, and two blocks back from the cops. She'd picked up a dinner shift at a restaurant and as Tony saw her, Angie was cashing out her apron, telling her manager she'd be on her way home for the night.

That put a grin on Tony's face. Like most of his friends on the island, she must have heard he was back by now. He ducked out before she saw him and made his way back to her place. He knew where the spare key was and he let himself in. The beer in the fridge wasn't his brand, which was strange and disappointing, but maybe it had been on special at the store. Sure. Maybe. He cracked one open and took a seat on a rattan chair in the dark living room, the ceiling fan with the banana frond blades spinning carelessly around and around.

He went through three of those damned beers before Angie walked in, humming softly to herself. She put on the light and that had Tony blinking rapidly to keep up.

"Tony! What in God's name are you doing here?"

He squinted as he stood, moving to her with his arms out. She cradled her own across her chest. "Looking for you, honey! What do you think I'm doing?"

She let him hug her but didn't respond, keeping her arms in the way. D'Amico grunted but gave way. "What is it, girl?" He didn't want to be the first to bring up the guy who'd been here earlier.

"You know the cops are looking for you."

"Yeah," he said, grinning again. "But they don't know I'm really here now, do they?"

Angie shook her head. "Maybe not. Knowing you, you're not exactly hiding."

"Ah, I'm not worried about the cops."

"You're on an island, Tony. Maybe you should be. You don't have anywhere to go."

Tony realized he was holding a beer can in his hand and drank deep. Then he laughed. "I can leave anytime I want." He stifled a belch. "But that's not the point. I've missed you, Angie."

The woman said nothing. Tony grew a little uncomfortable. He was still squinting, despite having had time to accustom himself to the light.

"Nothing?" he asked. "You haven't missed me at all?"

Angie moved further into the room, the initial spell of surprise broken. She dropped her keys on the kitchen counter and her bag on the second rattan chair.

"Sure I do, Tony. It's just—"

"It's just what?"

"It's just that I don't sit around waiting anymore. I need more than that." She lowered herself to the edge of the chair, in front of her purse.

"Oh, you mean like the—"

Tony didn't get the chance to finish. There was the sound of footsteps on the wooden staircase leading up to the door.

"Shit," Angie said. "You've got to hide yourself."

"No," said Tony. "I don't mind." His grin stretched wide across his face. "Really I don't."

Angie stepped across the room and grabbed his arm. "You don't understand. You have to. Come here."

For a moment he resisted, and then let go. He'd always liked her strength when she used her physicality to make her wants and needs known to him. "Get in the bedroom. Now." Her voice had changed to a hush as a knock sounded at the door. Tony opened his mouth but Angie didn't trust him. He'd had too many beers, she could smell them on him. She put her fingers over his mouth and turned him and saw him move to the slatted door. Then she spun around to answer the knock.

She knew who it was before she opened it. "Stefan," she said, pulling the door open and allowing the man to walk in. "What are you doing here?"

"Coming to see you, my sweetheart. You should be glad. I thought maybe we could—"

Angie didn't want him to finish that sentence. "You're too sweet. But you were just here this afternoon."

"And now I'm here again. What's the matter, baby? You don't think I can handle you this soon?"

It might be nice, she thought, but not like this. She went cold inside thinking what could happen at any second. "It's the other way around, honey. Sometimes a lady...."

From the bedroom Tony finished the beer in his hand. He wanted to vomit. Angie was his girl, had been for more than two years. And now this? Just who did she think she was protecting?

"Okay," Stefan said. "Okay. I can wait. We're looking for some guy now, may not even be here. Used to live on the island. All the locals know him." He

33

looked carefully at Angie. "Ever hear of this guy? Tony d'Amico?"

"Tony?"

"We've been going down Duval and hitting most of the places he could drink or eat. Some of the people that are talking, they say that you and d'Amico—"

Tony took his hand off the doorknob, changing his mind. This punk Stefan was a cop. This was why Angie wanted to stash him. Good girl, Angie.

"Yeah, I know Tony."

"Seen him lately?"

"No," said Angie. "Not for a few months. Three, four months, something like that."

"Keep in contact?"

"Why are you questioning me? What do you think I'm involved with?"

Stefan's voice lightened. "Nothing, honey, nothing. I just got to ask, that's all. You guys ever talk on the phone, text, e-mail, that sort of thing?"

Angie sat down on her chair again. Looking across at where Tony had been sitting, she saw the two empty beer cans he'd left behind.

"Angie?"

"Um, no," she said. "I don't have a cell phone, you know that. Too much money. Everything I need is here, on the island."

She couldn't tear her eyes off those damned beer cans but she could tell Stefan was coming closer. "That includes me, baby," he said, his crotch close to her face.

She pushed it away with one hand and stood up, searching for his eyes. They were on hers as she moved her lips to his, giving him a light kiss. "I know."

Stefan swept his glance across the room, not stopping on anything, and said, "Okay, girlfriend. I've got to get back out there. I just wanted to follow up on what I'd been hearing."

"Are you going to catch him?" she blurted.

"D'Amico? Sure. We're on an island. Where can he go?"

From the bedroom Tony could hear a period of silence. What he didn't know was if Angie could be giving him up right now. She was sleeping with this guy, anything was possible. Only now, he really was trapped. The cop would be on him before he could get the bedroom window open or the glass broken and himself through it. Just how bad did Angie want to be done with him?

He waited.

After another minute, he heard the front door close. He knew this trick. He wasn't coming out of the bedroom until Angie opened that door. And if it was anyone else ....

The knob turned, the door pushed in, and Angie stood there, the shine of perspiration on her forehead. She turned and walked back to the living room.

"You didn't give me up—" Tony started.

She stopped and pointed to where he'd been sitting when she'd come home. He saw the two empties immediately.

"Crap," he said. "Did that asshole—"

"Don't start."

"Did this guy see them?"

"He didn't say."

Tony d'Amico was back on the street, stopping to talk with the people he knew, stepping into a few of the bars when he got thirsty or when someone else was buying. He didn't like the newer places, the joints that represented the "new" Key West. They were college student bars, spring breakers, and he liked the more traditional places, the ones that rightly or wrongly claimed links to piracy, smuggling, Hemingway, and the like. When your drink looked like a snow cone, he wanted to vomit it at an amusement park somewhere.

The cops were still in front of him but they'd be finished soon. He doubted they'd double back—why work that hard looking for a ghost? On the other hand, even those bastards may start picking up a rumor or two now that he'd been making his rounds. There was still some Key West in a lot of these people though and the cops might rightfully not be convinced by all of them.

Unless that one asshole, that Stefan—

What had Angie been doing with that son of a bitch?

He knew what she'd physically been doing with the bastard, but the why of it, that's what bothered him most.

There was a group of people that looked like two large families standing on a corner talking about the storm and what they should do about it: should they leave the island, leave the Keys, before they were stuck here? What if they were forced to evacuate, could they go where they wanted, or would they have to stay in some sort of shelter?

Tony almost stopped long enough to tell them there was nothing to worry about. The storm wasn't even going to make landfall. The news coverage was enough to panic a statue. He'd been in California when there'd been earthquakes. Even the smallest one prompted around the clock coverage where nothing knew was said for twenty-four hours after the initial tremor. The news had already happen*ed*, it was no longer happen*ing*. Give it a rest already. Now we have a mild depression in the Gulf, no threat to land, and the tourists are restless.

"Get the bleeding hell out!" Tony shouted, but they only glanced at him. Just another drunk local. And at this point, that was about right.

Tony ducked into a restaurant where he knew the bathrooms were in a building that was disconnected from the restaurant itself. He was dancing while it was occupied and he about put his fist through the door before some Hawaiian-shirt wearing asshole finally came out, drying his hands on his shorts.

When Tony was back on the sidewalk, things had changed. It was late now, really late. After one in the morning and the people had started to thin out considerably. But that wasn't it. There wasn't just one patrol car parked on the street in front of him. Tony counted four, both in front and behind, and as he watched, two police SUVs slowly made their way along Duval.

"Fucking beer cans," he swore and then did it again. "Fucking Angie. Screwing a goddamn cop."

It was time to leave. He was near enough to the Blind Monkey that he could say "so long" to Old Pete and have another beer for the road without too much risk, and as he ducked in there, half a dozen voices started in with, "Hey, Tony, the cops—"

"Yeah, they found what they're looking for. She was my girl first, you know. Pete! I think I need a beer."

D'Amico tried to tell a few more stories but while his friends drank his beer, they couldn't follow the jumps in his logic. Not that it mattered. The beer he bought saw to that.

The stars were gone, obscured by a thick layer of cloud. Flashes of lightning occasionally lit the air way off along the horizon to the south, and there was no moon. Tony knew it was time to go. There was no point in going back to Angie. The only good thing he thought about her now was that she hadn't turned him in when she had the chance. She'd betrayed him in a far deeper way.

Duval Street was behind him now and he moved to the white clapboard house with the blue shutters as quietly as he good. He found the rope he'd left that morning and pulled it gently until the prow of the kayak slid easily out from under the porch. Untying the rope, he dragged it the rest of the way by the nylon handle looped through its front, making sure the paddle was still bungeed along its side.

It was a fourteen-foot sit-on-top kayak, easy to use, just long enough for the ocean as long as the waves weren't too big. Tonight was perfect for it.

He dragged it when he could, carried it when he had to, but it was over fifty pounds which is cumbersome in this shape and damn heavy when he was this drunk. It only took him seven minutes but he got it down to the rocky shore and pushed it into the water, scrambling after it. The water was bracing but growing up here he knew its smell, and its feel.

Tony walked the kayak out a little further, out into knee-deep water, where he unsnapped the paddle and straddled the craft before pulling his legs in. Even in the bag as much as he was, d'Amico didn't need a compass. He'd spent more time on the water than he had on interstate highways. He checked his markers to be sure of his bearings and dipped the paddle in the water.

And he was free.

The cops hadn't trapped him on the last bit of land in the Keys. No, Tony had led them to the last jumping off point in an ocean of water that could take him anywhere he chose to go. All he had to do now was make his rendezvous.

The air was thick around him, the night obsidian black but for the air-to-air lightning strikes in the far distance. Some storm. Tropical storm downgraded to a tropical depression. And the tourists were worried.

Ocean water made lapping sounds against the shell of the kayak as he paddled, and every so often he heard a bigger splash—a fish, a bird, a wave—nearby. Tony was perspiring heavily though he wasn't paddling hard, just steadily.

Too much beer, he knew. He felt his face form into his well-known grin. Well hell, he thought, I'm drunk!

There was something in the back of his mind, something about progress, although how could he tell in the dark, really? And then he saw the boat, its portside red light on the one end and the white light on the stern. His bearing was perfect; he was headed for the side of the boat.

His fears abated and d'Amico felt the tension from his shoulders relax as he continued to work his paddle. Another five minutes tops and he'd be at the boat, and from there he'd be gone. The car with the stuff in the trunk was as good as delivered, his own cut was already in his own stash, and he'd gotten to see Angie again, though that hadn't worked out like he'd hoped. The hell with her, the little bitch. He'd thought about taking her with him, but after she'd been with a cop? She was poison.

Tony stabbed at the water harder than he should as more lightning shook out above him, closer maybe, but still staying in the air. He bit down with his jaw and worked that paddle like he'd wanted to work on that prick Stefan, worked on that paddle like he'd wanted to work on Angie, though in an entirely different way. He punished both water and paddle until he knew he had to be just about to the boat, his back and shoulders aching. He looked up.

The boat wasn't any closer. If anything, it seemed it may have been further away.

What the hell, Tony thought, and started paddling again, the sweat pouring off his head and torso, this time his eyes not leaving the boat.

The hell's going on? he thought. I see the lights on both ends. It's not like it's moving sideways away from me. Hell, the damned thing's got to be anchored bow and stern out here.

Tony paddled as hard as he could though he could feel his strength ebbing. He'd already gone too hard too long. He lifted the paddle, blinked the sweat out of his eyes. As he bobbed along on the gentle swells, he thought he could sense himself moving further away from the boat.

"What the hell—" Tony thought, now bending over and trying to use his legs while he paddled. He had to get to that boat, at least get close enough so that he could call to them for help, or so they could see him and reach out.

Trying to involve his legs helped his back but it didn't help his stroke. During one pullback he struck the shaft against his knee and he kicked out, sitting back sharply. Just like that the kayak rolled and Tony was pitched into the black water.

The kayak, he thought, spitting a mouthful of bitter seawater. He reached out madly and struck its overturned body with his left hand. Relief. Kicking his legs, he maneuvered his body to the center of the shell and took a deep breath. Closing his eyes, he slipped beneath the water and drove upwards against one edge of the craft, following it as he surfaced and clutching at it again before it could drift away from him.

It was further than he expected but he swam in the direction he knew he had pushed it, only starting to think what would happen if he was wrong, if he couldn't find it. But two strokes later he was into the kayak and pulling himself back on top, wiping the lank hair from his face.

The paddle....

He could see the lights of the boat still, further away and off to his right, but he had lost his paddle and had no way to get there. Not that it had been going well even when he had the damned thing.

D'Amico felt a belch start from his stomach but something made him turn his head aside at the last moment that kept the vomit from splattering the front of him.

Shit, he thought. I'm way too damned drunk for this. Way too damned many beers. When did I get so freaking old?

He tried to work his way forward onto his stomach so he could use his hands like a surfer does when he paddles his board out to the waves, but the kayak was too high off the water. The more he tried the more the uneven surfaces hurt his ribs and chest and the unsteadier the kayak seemed.

Tony sat back and laughed. He was exhausted. Still drunk, his muscles were shot, his brain couldn't come up with a single plan other than trying to swim for the boat, and all he felt like doing was leaning back and closing his eyes.

He watched a few lightning flashes before he saw Angie's face before him. She was saying something about two empty beer cans....

The tidal surge produced by Tropical Storm Carter had been a fluke concurrence of several factors, including the normal cycle of the moon, the position of the sun, and the rotation of the Earth. This can cause a "king tide," or a perigean spring tide, and is usually predictable. But when T.S. Carter sucked up a bunch of water as it passed into the Gulf of Mexico, its deterioration into a tropical depression released that water into the king tide that lead to an onrush of water unlike any Key Westers could remember.

In the light of the dawn, two patrol sergeants from the Key West Police Department responded to a call about a vagrant sleeping in a kayak in the back yard of a private hotel property. When they checked his pockets, they found a driver's license with Anthony d'Amico's name on it.

"Hey," said the cop who'd found it. "I think this is the guy they were looking for last night."

"Guess they weren't looking in the right place," said his partner. "Let's get him in. Looks like the weather might turn to hell."

When Tony came to in the back of the patrol car, a blanket around his shoulders, he said, "Aw, shit," and vomited again. Behind him, the tides began to recede gently into the ocean as T.S. Carter dissipated and the named storm became rain. It fell on the island because it had nowhere else to go.

4

Escape

Albert L. Kelley

They say you can't see it, but the dull metal was clear.

It hasn't been easy, but I'm not one to complain. I grew up in Bahama Village, the part of Key West they don't show the tourists. It's a good neighborhood filled with Conch families who have lived there for generations. Although the neighborhood is changing, it still represents the poorest section of town. For years, efforts have been made to gentrify the neighborhood. Some city leaders wanted to turn it into a suburb of Miami. Businesses like Blue Heaven came in to open the place up to tourists. But they don't get past Petronia Street. Johnson's Café, which used to sell the best conch fritters in town, closed, torn down and was rebuilt as La Creperie; Santiago's Bodega is known for its tapas menus. But kids like me don't go to places like that. The rest of Bahama Village feels too dangerous for tourists to walk through. It still has its share of drug dealers operating openly in the streets. Nearly a quarter of the residents are in poverty and almost half have dropped out of school. Most of the houses are over eighty years old and show every day of those years. The effort of day to day living took priority over paint and repairs. If a roof leaked, a bucket would catch the water. If a window broke, a trash bag would seal it. Even houses that should be condemned were still lived in. Key West is expensive enough; home repairs can wait. In my house, five people lived in a two-bedroom house. My grandmother had one bedroom and had filled the rest of the house with statues of her saints. The other bedroom was for my parents. My brother and I slept in the living room.

Even home life takes a back seat to expenses. My parents put their life savings into getting my older brother through school. Once he got out he never came back. By the time I came along, they were just trying to get by. Not that they didn't try to do right by me, but my father had to work two jobs, so I rarely saw him. Mom's job let her be home for dinner, but she spent most of her free time with friends. I was pretty much left to fend for myself; even when I was in elementary school. In the suburbs I would be called a latch key kid, but we didn't have locks that needed keys. We didn't have anything worth locking up. Here I was just street.

After a few years I guess the stress of living got to my parents. A night didn't go by that they weren't fighting. It didn't matter what the reason was. Dinner was too hot; dinner was too cold. The TV was too loud. Sometimes there was no reason. Sometimes they would yell at me. Mostly my father. In fact, almost every argument started with him. Most times they would end with him too. Eventually he must have gotten tired of the fights as he started staying out later and later and then eventually, he just didn't come home at all. I guess I should have missed him but I didn't. I don't think Mom did either.

Once Dad left, Mom moved into Grandma's bedroom and I got my own bedroom for the first time. Most nights Mom and Grandma would be found on the porch socializing with the neighbors while the old men played dominoes nearby. There were a lot of kids in Bahama Village and we spent the evenings playing tag or chasing chickens. It made us fast. If we actually caught a chicken, it became dinner. Key West is known as a baseball town, but not for us. There aren't any baseball fields in Bahama Village. We played ball in the streets and our neighbors sacrificed a few windows. And when a window broke, we would all run. We never got caught, but they always knew who did it. We didn't have any pets because the local strays belonged to all of us. We fed them scraps from the trash and played fetch with sticks off the ground. It was a carefree life for a child although not the life many people would want.

There also is no elementary school in Bahama Village. We were bussed to Glynn Archer. Glynn Archer was a large concrete building with a giant steel tiger out front. It's located in the middle of old town, only a mile away from my house, but I never felt like I belonged in that neighborhood. The surrounding houses looked nothing like mine. They were larger, nicer. My family could never afford one of those.

As I moved into middle school, I became more of a street kid. There was nothing to do at home and the street offered freedom. I spent my days at Horace O'Bryant Middle School, my afternoon at Douglas Gym and my nights below the streetlights. I wasn't big on school, but I really had fun at Douglas Gym. There was always something to do there- basketball, tag, dodge ball. The people who worked there always tried to find things to keep us busy. During the summer I could be found at the community pool. The Martin Luther King Jr. Community Pool was just down the street from my house and was a great way to keep cool during the summer days. There is also an athletic park right next to the pool, so we would often play basketball there and then cool off in the pool afterwards.

You know the phrase, "It takes a Village"? Well, that Village was Bahama Village. Every kid was everyone's kid. We ate at whatever house we happened to be near, and we were punished by whatever adult happened to catch us. There were a lot of people who watched over us kids. We couldn't get away with nothing, there were so many eyes on us. By eighth grade, HOB was becoming a smaller part of the equation. I knew I was supposed to go to school each day; I just didn't feel like it. Homework was piled on, but I rarely did it, preferring instead to play with my friends. My mother and grandmother were too busy to pay attention to what I was or wasn't doing. While they wanted a better life for me, they didn't see school as a necessity. And they knew they couldn't afford to send me to college even if I did get through. Most of the people they knew had dropped out. None had gone to college. We didn't have a phone, so the school never bothered to tell them when I was skipping. When I did go to school, I found myself in trouble. I got into a few scuffles with the kids who felt they were privileged. They looked down on me, but to tell the truth, I looked down on them. They wouldn't last a day in my world. If I had to fight, I always made sure to do it when there were no teachers around. Still, I had plenty of meetings with the "School Resource Officer". Somehow I made it to high school; probably because they didn't want me back at HOB.

I was actually proud to go to Key West High School. Neither of my parents had graduated and for a while I saw it as a way out. It was a fairly new building as the old school had been severely damaged during a hurricane. The new school resembled a prison. It was essentially five concrete buildings surrounding a central courtyard. The only thing it was missing was barbwire on top the chain-link fence. I enjoyed my classes at Key West High School better than the classes at HOB, but I still enjoyed my freedom more. I wasn't too involved in outside school activities. I wasn't the greatest athlete so I didn't try out for any sports. And without a car or parents to drive, it was too difficult to be involved in any after school events. Although it felt a little imposing, my grades improved with the help of some good teachers.

In the 10th grade, I met my best friend James. James family lived in Poinciana Plaza, a public housing complex on the opposite side of the island from Bahama Village. It used to be military housing but was bought by the City to provide affordable homes. James was raised by a single mother who had failed her third trip to rehab and had just given up. His father had left her once he found out she was pregnant. She let James do whatever he wanted. He pretty much was raising himself. Even though he was too young to have a license, he would routinely borrow his mother's car and we would go joy riding. He taught me to drive out on Boca Chica Road when we should have been in science class. We found new places to hang out where the police wouldn't find us. Although we knew that if they did there was not much they could do. When students cut class, they just give them detention and then tell their parents. They couldn't even reach our parents so we didn't care.

James also introduced me to drinking. It wasn't something I really cared about. I preferred milkshakes and soda. But one day James smuggled a bottle of wine out of his mother's house. We drove the car to the bridle path by Smather's Beach and drank the whole thing. James liked drinking more than I did, but I didn't want him to drink alone. He got a fake ID and found a store that let him buy beer. While the other students were going to the football games on Friday night, we were drinking beer on Duval Street. When the cops came around, we would stash the drinks so they never caught on. Of course, I don't think the cops really cared. Usually they just hung out on the street corner across from the Bull in case something bad happened. We would harass the tourists as they walked by and flirt with all of the pretty girls. It never paid off, but we had a great time. Even on days we went to school, James usually had a six-pack in the car, or maybe a bottle of wine. Truthfully, I don't know where James got it all, but he found a way. I'm sure the teachers knew when we were toasted, but nothing was ever said. They probably just wanted to get us through the day. It wasn't long before we had scored our first bag of weed and found a better reason to cut class. We got through the first couple of years of high school, but I don't know how. As we started eleventh grade I began debating just dropping out. There wasn't much sense in going forward. I wasn't college material and I sure wasn't planning on joining the military. My future was not bright and I expected I would just be another unemployed Key Wester trying to get by.

James and I soon began experimenting with other substances, some good, others not so much. Coke and pills, mostly. I wasn't into things like needles so I stayed away from that stuff. I enjoyed getting high but never let it take over my life. But the down side was always the cost. It's not easy for unemployed high school kids to afford the "better" things in life when their parents are not affluent. Hell, ours weren't even fluent.

I tried getting a job but finding work in Key West when you are a teenager is nearly impossible. The only places hiring are fast food restaurants and clothing stores, but none of the clothing stores would hire a guy like me and I sure didn't want to flip hamburgers for eight dollars an hour. I took to selling stuff I owned, but I didn't own much. Even my parents didn't own much. Occasionally I could sneak as buck or two out of my dad's wallet, but he had so little it was risky. One day while walking down Truman Ave. I saw a bike leaning against the wall of a building. It didn't even have a lock on it. I jumped on and started riding fast. I made the first corner so if the owner came out he wouldn't see me. I peddled quickly to James's house. He had a can of paint so we quickly changed the bike's color. Once dry, we found a buyer for our "Conch Cruiser" and pocketed a nice profit. This started a whole new enterprise for us. And we got good at it. With a cheap pair of tin snips we could cut through most bike locks chains and soon learned we could pick most U-locks with a ballpoint pen. We never took bikes from Bahama Village, as those families needed everything they owned. We also never stole any on Duval St. where there would be witnesses. We preferred to go around Old Town on the back roads where we wouldn't be seen. We got to know which buildings had security cameras and avoided them. But you can only take so many bikes and make so much. We started going out to places like Key Haven at night to check the doors of the cars. If they were unlocked, we would grab whatever was on the seat or center console and run. Usually we didn't get much- phone chargers, or a few coins. But occasionally we would find a purse or wallet and get a few bucks. Once I even found over a grand. I bet someone had a hard time paying their bills that month. I never felt bad for them. If they could afford to live there, they could afford to lose a few bucks. But still, we never hit it big. We were dealing in small change. That's when James came up with the idea of cars.

He learned of a guy in Miami that would buy hot cars. I wasn't up for it at first. The problem with committing a big crime in Key West is the escape. There is only one road in or out and it is 120 miles long. That's a long way to go without getting caught.

Escape

Two days later James pulls up in a strange car. "Get in" he said. We drove to his house and he gave me his mom's keys. "Follow me." I started his mother's car and he led me to a dirt road in Rockland Key that I never knew existed. At the end of the road he stopped. He told me he found the car with the keys in the ignition. We left it there and drove back to town in his mom's car, stopping by Strunk's to get some paint. The next morning, we went back to Rockland and repainted the car, just like we had repainted the bicycles. We then went back into town after taking off the license plate. In town we swapped the plates with another car. I didn't sleep well that night anticipating the drive to Miami. In the morning we returned to Rockland to find the paint had dried, but with it were bugs and leaves and dust. As long as no one looked too close, the camouflage should work. James got behind the wheel and again I followed in his mother's car. We had discussed driving methods. I told him not to speed because he didn't want to get pulled over. It was probably the longest drive I ever made. It took us nearly four hours to reach the chop shop in Hialeah. But after all was said and done, we both walked away with a grand in our pockets.

We knew it wouldn't always be so easy, or occur so frequent. But we started looking for opportunities. And they were there. We found ways of lifting keys and found other hiding areas even closer to home. We were taking one to two cars a month and the profits started getting higher. We found Duval Street was a prime shopping area. If a tourist left his car unlocked, we would usually have several hours before they came back for it. By the time they finished drinking, the car would already be in pieces in Miami. We were making a pretty good living for a couple of teens.

Our fate was sealed after about six months. James found the car at the South end of Duval where we rarely went. After getting it to the designated hiding area near my house, we searched the car. Usually we would only pick up a few extra dollars, but this time it was different. Under the driver's seat we found a loaded pistol. Don't ask me what kind; I had never seen one before. James put it in his waistband. In the glove box was an envelope with ten thousand dollars. In the trunk we found bags of coke. At least a dozen of them. This was serious and far more than we had bargained for. We knew we had just crossed a line that couldn't be uncrossed. It was too late to take the car back and we knew the owners would be searching for it already. We had to move fast. We figured it wouldn't be reported stolen so we didn't have to paint it. But we couldn't deliver it to Miami with the cash and coke. We split the cash. I don't know what James did with his, but I put my share under my mattress in my bedroom. We stashed the coke in James's mother's car and started driving. We kept to our plan: James drove the stolen car and I followed behind in his mother's car. I kept close to him for the long drive. We got to Big Pine Key and I started to stress out over the 35 mile an hour speed limit. I wanted this drive to end but we didn't dare speed. The risk was too high. Another 35 mile an hour zone in Marathon and then we could start moving faster. The whole drive I thought about what we would do when we returned. I liked coke as much as the next guy, but that was too much for personal consumption. It was also a sure thing that the owners would be looking to see if any new dealers hit the street. Our best bet would be to find a buyer in Miami and unload it there.

My thoughts consumed me all the way to the 18-mile stretch. I started to relax. 65 miles an hour to the turnpike and then 75 miles per hour to the shop. I felt like we were almost there. Traffic was light and as anxious as I was, I wasn't prepared. When we reached the passing lane, a dark colored car passed me on the right clearly doing at least eighty miles an hour. As the car went to pass James, it swerved and hit the front quarter panel of the stolen car, slamming James into the protective wall that separates the northbound and southbound lanes. James spun to a stop right below a streetlight, blocking me from going forward. Dazed, James opened his door with the gun in his hand and ran towards me. He never felt the bullet that went through the back of his head. As he fell, the gun slid towards the driver's door of his mother's car. I wanted to hit reverse, but another car was blocking me from behind. Scared, I opened the door and reached for the gun. I don't know why; I had never fired one before. As I lifted it, I looked in front of me and saw two men walking my way, pistols pointed at me. I froze. I couldn't look away; I couldn't move. I heard a bang and saw the glint of dull metal flying towards me.

5

Nature Called

Justin Maxwell
(a/k/a Wayne "Skip" Kadar)

Will Mellard is a serial killer who is crisscrossing America practicing his own brand of selective elimination. He seeks out people who he determines are a menace to society. Specifically, people who take pleasure in hurting others; wife abusers, child molesters, white collar criminals who destroy the lives of their employees, and sometimes he kills people just because he doesn't like them. In a twist of irony, Will also murders murderers.

On a beautiful sunny day, Will was driving a rented Mustang convertible down US1 towards Key West. He was admiring the view from the Seven Mile Bridge; the Gulf of Mexico on the right and the aqua blue water of the Atlantic to his left. He drove with one hand on the steering wheel while the other was turning on his cell phone to take a photograph. Concentrating on pressing buttons, he was startled when a white

Cadillac suddenly came up on him fast from behind with its horn blaring.

Will quickly looked up from his phone and saw he had veered left and was straddling the center line taking up both north and southbound lanes. Fortunately, there wasn't any oncoming traffic. He quickly moved to his lane and the Cadillac swung out to pass. The driver floored his car to emphasize his anger. Will looked left at the car with an apologetic expression. But when the white Cadillac with a Rhode Island license plate and a New England Patriots bumper sticker flew by, Will saw the man giving him the finger.

"You scared the shit out of me. Screw you, asshole!" Will shouted shaking his fist with a raised middle finger as the white car disappeared in the distance.

Will checked the rear view mirror, and finding no other vehicles behind him, slowed down again to appreciate the tropical paradise of the Florida Keys.

In Key West, Will partook of all the normal tourist activities. He drank a beer at Sloppy Joe's and Hog's Breath, ate a cheeseburger in paradise at Margaritaville, and took a ride on the Conch Train. He had heard about the sunset celebration held at Mallory Square each evening and was anxious to join that party like atmosphere.

As he walked down Duval Street towards the waterfront, Will stopped to look in the store windows selling anything from 3 for $10.00 tee shirts to gallery quality art, from dope smoking paraphernalia to luxurious jewelry. He listened to live music blaring from the open air establishments, and he was amazed to see people walking down the street openly carrying cups of beer.

At Mallory Square, where the cruise ships dock and regurgitate thousands of tourists onto the small island, Will found street performers setting up for the evening's sunset celebration. He sat on a bench and settled in to do some people watching and drink the beer he picked up at Captain Tony's Bar.

Mallory Square was beginning to fill with people, many wearing Royal Caribbean or Carnival Cruise Line stickers on their shirts, families escaping the cold Midwest winter, and couples and individuals of all ages. There were college students; many of the guys having consumed to excess and the girls parading around wearing the minimum. There were middle aged people, some acting and dressing as though they were re-living their younger years, and foreign tourists snapping pictures of the chickens and roosters freely roaming the city streets. However, it seemed to Will that the Baby Boomer generation represented the largest segment of the tourist population.

The beers had swelled Will's bladder to the point he needed to seek relief. He asked a City of Key West municipal worker emptying a trash can where the restrooms were.

The man pointed to a small building near the main entrance to the square. "See them people standing over dar? That be it."

Will looked at two lines snaking down the sidewalk. The line of men was long, and the women's line was even longer. "I don't know if I can wait that long," he mumbled.

The man laughed and said, "Know what ya mean brother, when nature calls ya gots ta answer. Not suppose to tell ya, but there's johns beyond them bushes. They private, for the construction crew workin on the new hotel, but the gate ain't locked. I use 'em all the time."

Will thanked the man, tossed his empty cup in the trash and walked toward the row of bougainvillea with deep red flowers.

As he approached the parking lot Will noticed a car double parked. It was a white Cadillac just like the one that blew by him earlier that day. He checked and the car had a Rhode Island plate and the same bumper sticker. The driver who flipped him off earlier was sitting in the air conditioning yelling at someone on the other end of his cell phone. Will's anger for the man began to once again boil.

The man exited his car with a slam of the door. He had watched a family of tourists open the gate to use the private portable toilets and decided to go in. Will followed the man through the gate to a row of four functioning blue plastic portable toilets and one with an "Out of Order" sign.

Will, the family and the man were the only people in line for the currently occupied facilities. One member of the family of four stood in front of each unit waiting for the red occupied signs on the doors to turn green and read unoccupied. Will stood in line patiently waiting his turn thinking of the time he and his mother went to the Missouri State Fair and his mother called these type of toilets plastic poop palaces.

An older woman wearing a tight fitting Schooner's Wharf Bar tee shirt and a straw cowboy hat walked out of the larger handicapped porta john. The young boy standing next in line, squirming in obvious urinary distress, started in but the Cadillac driver suddenly stepped in front of the boy and entered. Will watched and was pissed, and nothing good ever comes from pissing off a serial killer.

The door opened in the plastic cubical Will was next in line for but he motioned the boy to take his turn. Will stepped to his right to wait outside the handicapped unit.

The family completed the tasks at hand and departed the area of the little plastic enclosures, leaving only an asshole in the handicapped unit and an angry serial killer waiting outside of it.

When the door unlocked, changing the little sign to unoccupied and the door swung open, Will rushed in taking the man by surprise.

A few minutes later Will opened the door and exited. He took the "Out of Order" sign taped to the door of the defective toilet, stuck it on the handicapped unit and walked back to Mallory Square to watch a man balancing on a unicycle while juggling flaming batons.

The next morning several cars with flashing red and blue lights and an ambulance whose attendants didn't seem to be in a hurry filled the new hotel parking lot. Key West Police had cordoned off the portable toilets with yellow crime scene tape and twenty to thirty tourists looked on snapping pictures to post on their Facebook pages. Among the group was the serial killer, Will Mellard.

When the medical examiner arrived, she approached an officer and asked, "So, what do we have?"

"Dead guy in the handicapped portable toilet," he responded.

"Who was first on the scene?" she asked.

He answered, "I was."

"Did you attempt resuscitation?" the M.E. asked.

Writing notes in his small notebook he responded, "Huh? What? I didn't hear you."

Not happy she had to repeat herself she slowly asked, emphasizing each word, "Did you give the victim mouth to mouth resuscitation?"

"Hell no!" the officer replied emphatically.

"Why not?" she said, admonishing the cop. "Department policy states the first officer to respond at the scene of a person in destress must make an attempt to resuscitate the victim."

With a gloved hand, the officer opened the door of the handicapped portable toilet. The medical examiner looked inside the plastic enclosure, to see a man leaning over the stool. His head had been shoved down into the disgusting mixture of blue deodorizing liquid, urine, soggy toilet paper and floating turds.

The M.E. uttered, "Oh." She then looked at the officer and said, "I think we can rule out suicide."

6

Waiting for Jimmy Buffett

Barthélemy Banks

Tim Malloy sat on a barstool at Margaritaville, wondering if Jimmy Buffett would walk through the door. Wasn't very likely. Buffett owned the bar chain through a big conglomerate, Margaritaville Holdings LLC (a subsidiary of Cheeseburger Holding Company, LLC). He rarely came here. These days ol' Jimmy lived on the mainland, only occasionally visiting Key West, the island oasis that was the basis of his fame.

When the bartender delivered the fourth salt-rimmed drink, Malloy tried to tell himself he wasn't really a drunk, like so many of his compatriots sitting at the long wooden bar. He was just drowning his sorrows.

He had many. That's why he was hiding away in this end-of-the-road town. As the southernmost city in the continental United States, it was literally the end of US1 – nowhere left to go.

People said Cuba lay 90 miles to the south – closer than Miami to the north – but Malloy expected that wasn't true. Beyond the Florida Straits lay the edge of the world, where ships sailed over the rim never to be seen again. Just like in those old mariners' maps labeled "Here there be dragons."

At that very moment one of the dragons ambled in the door.

José Lupe was a Cuban who had worked for Castro's secret police, the Dirección General De Inteligencia. The agency was established with the help of the Soviet KGB in 1961, following Fidel Castro's rise to power.

Malloy knew José Lupe from his former life, when he had been an assassin for the CIA. But that had been long after Operation MKRIFLE, the agency plot to kill Castro. The failed attempts ranged from exploding seashells to poison pills to lining his diving suit with a toxic chemical. Even the Mafia had pitched in, to no avail.

José had been there by Castro's side in those bad old days. Malloy came to the CIA later, long after John F. Kennedy was dead from Lee Harvey Oswald's bullets and Fidel and Raul were basking under a non-invasion policy that came out of the so-called Cuban Missile Crisis.

Malloy had actually worked with José Lupe back in '98, when they took out a Colombian who was trying to corner the sugar market. Neither Cuba nor the US wanted that.

"Hello, M," said José as he slid onto the barstool next to Malloy. M had been his cryptonym. Intelligence agencies liked to use codenames, Spy vs. Spy nonsense.

"Hi there, Georges." That was José's cover name, going back to when he worked under cover in Key West, spying on the CIA who was spying on Cuba. The CIA had a big listening station just inside the gates of the Navy base off Whitehead Street. You could recognize it by all the antennae. Operatives monitored Cuban radio stations and whatnot from there. Hush-hush stuff. So the erstwhile Georges Hernandez had managed a stand that sold coconut milk to tourists there at the Southernmost Point monument, maybe a hundred yards from the CIA listening station.

"How many drinks you had?" asked José, ordering one for himself.

"Not enough."

"Slow down. We need to talk."

That got Malloy's attention. What business did this old spy have with a put-out-to-pasture shooter? M hadn't been on the payroll for several years now. He'd been deemed unreliable after his partner ran away with his wife and he'd replaced her with the bottle.

Wasn't fair, Malloy thought. His hand hardly shook. He could still hit a target at three inches, that being the usual distance between him and a target's head. (Target was fancy spy-talk for victim.)

"What's on your mind?" said Malloy, finishing off his drink and signaling for a fifth. No need to look too interested.

"Somebody's trying to kill me. I need your help."

Malloy looked up. "Last I heard, you and I are on opposite sides."

"We've worked together before," the Cuban referred to the Colombian sugar king. "Besides, we're in the same business. Call it professional courtesy."

Malloy frowned. "We're not in the same business. I'm retired. At your age, surely you are too." Having been around for the Cuban Missile Crisis, José Lupe had to be 75 if he was a day.

"You'll want to help me on this. You're a target too. The Colombians."

"Sugar growers would try to kill us?"

"We killed their guy. Why not? Sugar is big business. That why we got that assignment twenty years ago."

The idea of the CIA and the Cuban DGI working together was unheard of. Not that it hadn't happened. It was just unheard of – secret, that is. When the two countries had common interests (like the sugar market) they found ways to bend the rules.

"Me? I'm a ghost. No longer involved in that world."

"Ghost maybe. But you used to be a spook. The Colombians have long memories. Apparently a nephew of our target has risen through the ranks and now has the power to take revenge."

Malloy swiveled to face the elderly Cuban. "So, what do we need to do to put a stop to this?"

"Two things. Stop the assassin assigned to take us out. And kill the nephew. Him gone, nobody will care."

Malloy finished off his fifth drink. Taking out a professional assassin and a security-cocooned sugar baron would be a challenge. Hell, he didn't even have a gun.

"Do you have a plan," Malloy asked.

"Divide and conquer. You take out the shooter on our tail. And I'll go for the nephew."

"Why do you get the nephew?"

"I speak better Spanish than you do. A gringo would stand out in Colombia. You'd never get within ten miles of *El Sobrino*."

"Fair enough." Malloy set his salt-freckled glass on the bar. "Gotta go to the john. Be right back."

"*Sí*, take a piss, then come back and we'll work out the details."

Malloy weaved through the crowded tables toward the back. The restrooms were up some stairs and around a corner. He didn't look back over his shoulder to see if the man in the combat boots was following him. He knew he would.

As Mallory passed a table just before the hallway next to the stage, a dark passageway that led to the stairs, he snagged an empty wine bottle off an empty table awaiting bussing. He slid it under his loose Tommy Bahama shirt, holding it with his left arm, against his ribs.

When he entered the men's room, he stepped into the toilet stall but didn't latch the plywood door. He stood there, waiting, wine bottle now in his hand. When he heard somebody come into the restroom, he swung the stall door open and swung the bottle like a handball paddle.

Whak!

The bottle didn't shatter, but the Latin man's cranium may have. Malloy swung the bottle again.

Whak!

The man was down.

Whak!

The man was dead.

Malloy wiped the bottle with a paper towel, then tossed it in the trash bin. He hoisted the Latin man under his armpits and dragged him into the stall. After placing him on the toilet seat, he locked the door from the inside, then crawled out under the stall wall. There was barely enough room, but Malloy had always been good at limbo dancing. In this case, he slivered like a snake.

When he sat down beside José Lupe, he said, "Okay, I've done my part. Now you go take care of *El Sobrino*."

"What?"

"The shooter's dead. Just dispatched him in the john."

José's eyes bulged. "You just killed a man?"

"Wasn't hard. Remember, like you, I'm a trained professional."

"¡*Dios mío*! Are you sure you got the right *sicario*?"

Malloy knew enough Spanish to recognize *sicario* as meaning hitman or hired assassin. Lingua franca, you might say. "Well, he was carrying this," he said, pulling up his Tommy Bahama enough to reveal the butt of a Ruger LCP .380 sticking out from under his waistband. A nice semiautomatic pistol with fixed sights on a 2-inch barrel, glass-filled nylon grips for a secure grasp, and a magazine that held six rounds.

"That would do the job if you're up close."

Malloy shrugged. "The bathroom upstairs is pretty small." He laid out two photographs on the bar – images of a younger José Lupe and himself in a crew-cut. "He had these on him too."

"Hmm, no doubt about him. But how did you spot him?"

"Came in after you. Wore combat boots that looked like military issue. Kept staring at us from a table near the window. Tourists who sit by the window watch the parade of people moving down the sidewalk. Pretty girls in halter-tops. Gay guys with eyeliner. Freaks wearing purple Mohawks. Motorcycle dudes sporting heavy mustaches and black leather jackets. Their girlfriends wearing studded collars and displaying acres of skin with intricate tattoos. Not something you'd ignore unless you were focused on something more important – like us."

"I must be getting old. I didn't spot him."

"Your back was turned."

"All the worse. One always watches his back."

"Have a good trip."

"Trip? *¿De qué estás hablando?*"

"You're going to Colombia, remember? Your side of the deal."

"*Sí*, I must be going." He stood up, fumbling in his pockct for his wallet. The imprint of a pistol showed against his shirt. He had gained too much weight in recent years, making his shirts too tight to properly conceal a weapon.

"Don't worry about the margarita. It's on me. I appreciate the tip about *El Sobrino*."

"*De nada*. I will send you a postcard from Colombia. I know your post office number."

When he saw my surprise, he said, "I still have resources. Now that Fidel and Raoul are gone, information flows more freely."

"Travel safely."

"*Sí, muchacho*. I will do that."

Two months later, Malloy received a postcard covered in the colorful stamps of a foreign postal service. The card pictured a colorful city, the small print identifying it as Bogotá. On reverse, an ink scrawl read: EL TAZÓN DE AZÚCAR ESTÁ VACÍO. LA MISIÓN HA SIDO CANCELADA.

Translation: THE SUGAR BOWL IS EMPTY. THE MISSION (HIT) HAS BEEN CANCELED.

Georges had kept his part of the bargain. And added a sweetener.

7

Soulmates

R. K. Simpson

I was sipping a coke at the Orlando Airport, waiting to board my flight back to Boston, when I glanced at the television and saw her face for the first time in more than twenty years. The mug shot made her look considerably older than I, but that was a picture of my high school girlfriend, I was quite sure. Then, over the din in the bar, I heard the newscaster say, "Ms. Chloe MacLaren, the dead man's daughter, is a person of interest in the case." Hearing that news was shocking, but deep down I was not entirely surprised.

When I knew Chloe, two internal forces seemed to be battling to control her. The dominant Chloe was difficult to know and impossible to understand. She operated on impulse much of the time, which made her unpredictable. She disliked schedules, did not make lists, and never wore a watch. This Chloe was an introvert who disliked people, but had developed an extraordinary ability to manipulate them. She could make a positive impression on the most skeptical and discerning, and always got what she wanted, one way or the other.

The subordinate Chloe fought constantly to keep her humanity from being trampled. Because she loved animals, especially horses, she had volunteered at a large-animal clinic since she was fourteen. The same protective instinct drove her to look after her friends. In my case, throughout our senior year she never missed an opportunity to point out why I needed a college education. She is, no doubt, the primary reason I now have a Master's degree in Spanish and have been able to find work easily. She even talked her father into lending me money to pay school bills when funds from my scholarships and work were insufficient.

I liked her father, Jock MacLaren, from the first time I met him. Known to all as Scotty, he was a man of few words and subtle wit. After watching one of Florida's long-winded governors on television, he shook his head, fixed me with those piercing blue eyes, and said, "Remember, you never learn anything when you're talking." At 5' 6", he stood ramrod straight on bowed legs. He had close-cropped red hair, an aquiline nose, and small blue eyes that looked into you, not at you. He was smart and shrewd and if anyone could have figured out his daughter, it was he. But those two strong-willed, stubborn, personalities were a volatile mix. One word could spark an argument between them and sometimes it did. It was a damned shame.

I had never spoken to Chloe until the first day of our senior year when Fate dropped me into a chair right behind hers. She was wearing a yellow sundress that revealed toned and tanned arms and shoulders and enough of the tops of her breasts to make me hope every morning she would wear that dress again. Her reddish-brown hair was cut boyishly short and her nose was too long for her face, but her beautiful eyes drew attention from it. Their delicate color seemed to change from grey to green to grey-blue depending on her surroundings. And like a cat's eyes, they saw everything and revealed nothing.

As soon as I sat down, Chloe turned around in her seat, extended her hand, and said, "You're Sandor Rigor, right? Do you prefer Sandy?"

"Either," I said.

Despite having little in common, I think she selected me to be her senior-year toy that morning. We were so different that some kids referred to us as "the odd couple." Chloe was a member of the in-crowd, while I stayed as far from that group as I could and indiscriminately disliked every kid in it. Chloe's family had money; we had none. Chloe was a diligent student motivated to do her best always. I was a lackadaisical, unmotivated, pain-in-the-ass student. The teachers who knew me considered me an under-achiever because, according to the IQ test we took at the beginning of our sophomore year, mine was an impressive 130. Chloe did not consider me an under-achiever, however, which was more important to me, because from the first time we slept together we were in perfect synch.

We did share one other thing, something that was much less common then than it is now: each of us was an only child being raised by a single parent. We believed we were the only ones in school who understood how difficult the loss of a parent was, how far-reaching and long-lasting the loss was, and how strong the urge was to be just normal kids again. We felt a powerful bond and believed that surviving all we had made us soulmates.

~ ~ ~

Several weeks after seeing Chloe's face on the news, I received a call from a high school classmate. "Sandor, this is a voice from your past. Anthony Gonzalez. Remember me?"

"Yes, of course, Anthony. Que pasa, amigo?"

"Well, you know, it's about Scotty's...death," he stammered. "My dad used to work for Scotty. He really idolized him. He told great stories about Scotty all the time at home. After high school, when I didn't know what I wanted to do and didn't have a job, Scotty hired me to work in the stables. He talked to me often about life and problem-solving and he helped get me pointed in the right direction. To tell you the truth, his death has really been difficult for me." He paused, took a deep breath and continued. "Then, I remembered that you knew him quite well too, and thought it would be good to talk to you." Anthony's answer left me waiting for more explanation and more candor.

"Yes, I knew him well," I said, without elaborating. "What can you tell me about his death, Anthony?" I asked.

"Well, here's what I know for sure. He died when he was thrown from his horse, Lucky. There were rumors that he had had some heart troubles. Maybe he had a heart attack; maybe he should not have been

riding. I'm not sure. I do know that a female friend of Chloe was riding with them that morning. And lastly, I know the press is beginning to publish all kinds of unsubstantiated shit. My father says that's what happens when rich men die."

"How much was he worth? Any idea?"

"That guy just had a knack for making money, Sandor. One article estimated he was worth twenty million.

"Holy shit!" I blurted. "So that's what she inherited?"

"I don't know, but that's generally the way it works. She's an only child. Now she's a rich only child."

"Is there something I can do for you, Anthony?"

"No, not really," he said, unconvincingly. He hesitated and I waited. Finally, he said, "Look, if Scotty was killed, I would hate to see the murder covered up. I know you are smart and I thought you might feel like I do. That's all. If I can do anything, let me know. I know some people."

"Comprendido," I said. "Don't worry, Anthony, we're on the same wavelength. I can feel it. Would you mind sending me the articles you mentioned that were full of rumors?" I asked.

"Absolutely. I've saved them all and I'll send you new ones as I see them."

"And it might be helpful if you could confirm the heart rumors and find out the name of Chloe's friend who went riding with them that day?"

"I'll try, Sandor."

~ ~ ~

Anthony said two things that piqued my interest. First, he said Scotty had been bucked off his horse. While that was theoretically possible, in reality, it was hard to imagine. Everyone who worked on that ranch had been in awe of his horsemanship. He was strong, agile, and decisive, just what a horse needs to avoid disaster. Plus, Scotty had ridden Lucky for a decade. He knew her every mood and move, and Lucky knew if he had gained a pound or two or was wearing new boots. Anthony's story gave off a peculiar odor.

Second, I could not stop thinking of Chloe's twenty-million dollar inheritance. I sat there for some time in my one-bedroom rental unit, looking out my dirty front window at the traffic crawling along Route 29 and past a non-descript used car lot. God Almighty! Twenty million dollars!

I mused that if that amount ever fell into my hands, the first thing I would do would be take my mother house shopping. Then I would explain that working in the bar had just become optional. "Do whatever you want Mom," I would say. "You've earned it many times over." What a great feeling that would be!

My mother, Nancy Lancaster, had little education because around her tenth birthday, she started working in the vegetable and flower farms where her mother worked. She was a wholesome, blond, blue-eyed gal who, by the time she was in her mid-teens, found it easy to get work as a waitress. When she turned eighteen, she graduated to bartender, and that became her life's work. The pay seemed good to her when she started because she learned how to entice big tips and she could work until midnight most nights.

But those many years on her feet had contributed to her arthritic knees and back. The longer I thought about it, the more certain I was: it was time for my mother to live in her own place and treat herself to some rest and relaxation.

And so it was that I began to consider seriously the idea of siphoning off some of Chloe's grotesquely large inheritance for my mother – and me. As I began to weigh the risks involved, I realized my greatest concern – maybe fear – was Chloe. I felt that dread of intimidation return when I recalled her quick temper, her relentlessness, and her cold-hearted determination. If I went after her money, I would have to face those qualities and the fact that, ultimately, it would be me against her, no holds barred, winner take all. Could I force her to submit to me? To do my bidding? I had never been able to before, but I was so insecure back then that I had a recurring dream in which Chloe made me do things I knew were wrong or dangerous. We talked about it once and she admitted that she would love to have that kind of power over people because she would enjoy seeing how they reacted, especially to danger. She was frightening sometimes when she spoke her intimate little truths like that, but I was about to learn that her actions could be even more frightening.

The incident began Friday evening. We had gone to a pep rally for the high school football game the next day. I was so nervous I felt sick. I had promised myself I would tell Chloe I was not happy with our relationship. And so I did. Without any preamble, I said, "You're so demanding, Chloe. I try so hard to keep you happy that I'm not happy myself." I caught Chloe absolutely by surprise.

"What the hell are you talking about?" she shot back.

"I was attracted to you, like I was to the pep rally fire tonight," I told her, using a line I had thought up and rehearsed in bed the previous night. "If I saw an orange glow in the night sky, I would alter course and go to it; I couldn't help myself. It was like that when I met you. I was drawn to you. You were like a beautiful fire." Up to that point, she was listening, but then I said, "But now I feel I'm too close to you for my own good, that I have to keep my wits about me or you might draw me in one step too close to the fire and little Sandor would be nothing but ashes in the wind." In reply, she told me what I could do with my ashes, got out of my mother's ancient car, and slammed the door so hard I thought she had broken it.

I anticipated a long silence from Chloe and was surprised when she called on Sunday. She sounded fine and in the most courteous terms invited me to the ranch that afternoon to ride. It was the type of invitation you cannot easily turn down, so I accepted with the hope that we would find some time and privacy to continue our last conversation in a more civilized tone.

During most of the thirty-minute drive to the ranch, I thought about Chloe. Despite the material things her father's financial successes brought her, life had been lonely for her. She had lost her mother, Samantha, when she was fourteen months old to the most brutal killing that ever occurred in Kissimmee.

She was raped and murdered while walking home from the movies. Her killer was never found and Scotty – I am sure he would agree – never fully recovered.

For several weeks after Sam died, Scotty stayed in his house, spoke to no one, and contemplated suicide, recording his thoughts on this alternative solution in a small notebook he carried with him at all times. One morning before daybreak, he walked down the hall to his daughter's room, stood by her crib, and was entranced by her quiet, rhythmic breathing. He studied a wisp of blond hair that fluttered each time she exhaled, and he consciously absorbed every aspect of the peaceful expression on her face. He had no idea how long he stood there but at some point, he felt the tension in his neck lessen and the vice that had gripped his chest loosen slightly. Even the anger and sorrow that had caused his worst suffering began to diminish. During that time of solitude and contemplation, Scotty decided not to take his life.

He told me this story one evening driving home from a tennis tournament Chloe played in. These memories affected Scotty so deeply that he had to pull off the road and collect himself. I had to pull off at a gas station myself that morning on my way to the ranch because my mind was on Scotty and Chloe, not the road. I sat in the car with a cup of coffee and wished that all three of us could start again.

Scotty was thirty-five years old when Samantha died. He was already one of the wealthiest and most influential ranchers in central Florida, and he had just been elected President of the Florida Cattlemen's Union. For six months or more after his loss, Scotty struggled with depression. Mornings were the worst time of day. Often his first thought was 'Sam's gone.' This hit him so hard sometimes that he could not get out of bed. Other mornings he was awakened by the shattering thought that her killer was still on the loose and maybe lived around the corner where he was free to enjoy his life.

Of course time helped them heal. A year or two into her teens, Chloe's highs and lows began to even out, and she took up tennis and riding. Her athletic successes brought her social standing and confidence, but she remained edgy and demanding with Scotty. She just wanted to spend time with him, but it seemed to her that he always chose a meeting with a businessman over an ice cream with her. It made her furious that she could not control him, not even an hour of his day. In turn, her outbursts made him angry and exasperated and their relationship spiraled downward. By the time I arrived in her life, she was seventeen and was essentially estranged from her father. In one of our first serious conversations I remember Chloe saying, "I admire him in some ways, I really do, but I hope to God I don't turn out to be like him. A week later Scotty allowed me my first glance into the state of their relationship when he said, "I am already mourning her loss."

It is impossible to say what kept father and daughter apart. Perhaps it was some genetic disconnect or psychological block Scotty developed as a result of his wife's violent death. I believe Scotty cared for her deeply, although he could not always show it. Chloe, on the other hand, was as cold-blooded as a snake. I never saw Chloe demonstrate a need for human warmth or the ability to generate it.

I arrived at the MacLaren ranch that morning a little late for my riding date. I turned off the main road and onto two sandy grooves in the zoysia grass that ran for about half a mile between two rows of graceful Norfolk Pines. I saw her in the corral, bridle in one hand and blanket in the other, running after a big, black horse. When I pulled to a halt, she dropped the gear, jogged to the car, and said, "I'd like to put Friday behind us as fast as we can."

"Done," I replied, feeling cowardly. She bent down, extended her head and shoulders through the open window and kissed me on the lips. "Take that, cowboy," she grinned.

Shortly thereafter, while walking to the barn, Chloe said, "I think Tetu'll be a good horse for your first ride. He's young and very responsive." I knew next to nothing about horses, but I knew Tetu was a thoroughbred and, therefore, might be high strung, or easily spooked. At first glance he looked enormous. His coat, mane, and tail were jet black, and his opaque black eyes seemed to obscure his attitude and intentions.

Chloe gave me several pointers as she expertly put on his bridle, placed the bit in his mouth, and wrapped the reins around a hitching post. "A horse will move away from pressure," she said, as she threw a blanket over Tetu's back. "So, Rule #1 is: stay relaxed. Hands, arms, ankles, legs – all relaxed. If you're tense, he'll pick up mixed signals which could confuse him." As she spoke, she was trying to tighten the cinch around the horse's girth, but Tetu acted irritable and resisted Chloe's efforts.

"You little devil," she said to Tetu.

"What's the matter?" I asked.

"Well, Mr. Greenhorn, if the cinch isn't tight, the saddle will roll off his back and you'll roll onto on the ground. To make matters worse, Tetu has learned to inhale deeply just before I tighten the cinch. This expands his rib cage. After I have the saddle on him, he expels that air so the cinch won't be so tight. Pretty smart, eh?" But I have a trick of my own," she said. "Let's see if it works." With that she turned toward the horse's flank and drove her knee up into his belly so hard that he expelled a big whoosh of air. Simultaneously, Chloe tightened the cinch and Tetu laid his ears back, switched his tail, and gave Chloe a look that needed no explanation. But the cinch was tight and the saddle secure.

"Sorry," she said to me. "It didn't hurt him – just got his attention."

"You should apologize to him, not me," I suggested.

"You mount up now and let's see what happens," she said, with a touch of impatience in her voice As soon as i was seated. She handed me the reins.

"Wait a sec," I said, searching for the stirrups with the toes of my sneakers, but Tetu was moving. He walked briskly by the hitching post. Then, without warning, he was in a full gallop, flying around the corner of the barn. He missed driving my knee into it by a fraction of an inch. He banked hard to the left, shot along a fence and began to increase his speed. I have no idea what I did during our speed run, other than maintain my two-handed death grip on Tetu's mane. I do remember my breathing coming in ragged gasps. Suddenly Tetu veered away from the fence and, still at full speed, headed straight for the side of the barn. I was sure that in his crazed state he was going to run right through it. I tried to make myself small and crouch behind his head and neck, but about two feet from impact, he stopped short and I flew over his neck and head like a champagne cork exploding out of the bottle. I hit the barn back first and upside down.

Although I do not remember what happened next, on-lookers said I bounced to my feet instantly and threw a right cross with every ounce of strength available in me while letting out a hair-raising scream. The punch landed flush on the middle of Tetu's upper lip, one of the most sensitive parts of a horse's anatomy, I learned later. Tetu reacted to the pain, noise and surprise of it all by bucking and snorting like a rodeo bronc. Then he took several steps backward, whirled around and charged into the corral. I last saw him galloping away from me and thought, 'He's going in the right direction.'

My mouth was full of corral dirt. I also had a bloody nose and two sore wrists. Someone handed me a bucket of water and said, "Here, Sandy, wash your mouth out. You okay?" Then I heard an older hand say, "They shoulda sent that crazy bastard to the glue factory long ago! He's gonna kill someone."

Chloe walked up then and took over. "Okay, thanks folks, break it up – think we've got everything under control."

"Are you okay? Do you need to go to the hospital?"

"I'm okay, I think."

"How'd you like to go for a nice horseback ride?" she asked. I flashed her an unamused smile. "Let's go over to the house."

We sat in the living room, close but not touching, silent much of the time, brooding over what had happened and what might have happened. When I closed my eyes, images from the afternoon slid into and out of focus. The more I saw, the closer I came to reliving the entire incident. Chloe, the horse expert, had been dead wrong. Tetu was neither young nor responsive. I missed something she was saying, then tuned in again.

"... and I've cinched him that way for years."

The physical repercussions of the ride were making themselves known. I was nauseous and dizzy and felt like I was coming down with the flu. And I could not shake the image of those menacing empty, black eyes. "I've got to go, Chloe," I said and climbed off the sofa. "I don't feel so great." As I stood, all the fog suddenly blew away. All my questions had answers. "Holy shit!" I stopped and stared at Chloe.

"What?" she asked.

"You arranged that disaster, didn't you? It all makes sense now. You set me up, man! Your invitation. That big kiss. Making me ride that thoroughbred nut case and kicking him in the stomach just before you put me on his back. It was all thought out in advance. You could have killed me!" I grabbed her by the upper arm and jerked her so hard both her feet came off the floor. "I oughta kick your ass," I snarled.

"You don't have the cojones," she said. I watched as big tears ran down both sides of her face, but she made no noise. They were tears of anger not sadness. Then, POOF, the teenager was gone and an irrational woman was shouting at me. "You're nothing more than a little mama's boy, Sandor. You don't have the backbone to survive in this world. You little piss ant." I listened briefly, hoping she would pause so I could toss in my two cents, but she was gaining momentum and slipping beyond reason. So, I walked out the door and did not see her again until that day in the bar at the Orlando airport.

I never saw Scotty again either, although I did stay in touch with him. For over five years, we called each other regularly and talked about everything under the sun. It was as if he had found a son, and I, a father. The better I knew him, the more I liked him. The only aberration in our relationship was that neither of us ever mentioned Chloe.

~ ~ ~

Three days after our last phone call, an envelope arrived at my post office box full of speculative articles. The reporters must have had fun making up stories about Chloe's many affairs, her lost inheritance, and her role pushing illicit horse drugs. I did glean some useful nuggets from articles in the more reputable papers: Chloe had been a pro tennis player, had acquired three DWI's, and had changed her home address to 555 Padgett Circle in Ocala. As a

*bonus, Anthony had written "Gladys Montoya,
horsewoman," on a piece of paper and put it in the
envelope. No mention was made of Scotty's alleged
heart condition.*

~ ~ ~

The time had come to make a decision about the
possibility of relieving Chloe of some of her
inheritance. My preliminary thoughts swept away the
fantasy that somehow I could do this without breaking
the law. To supplement my income as a Spanish
language teacher, I had worked part-time as a bank
teller, as an assistant parole officer in a juvenile
detention center, and as an Emergency Medical
Technician. In those jobs I met folks who were familiar
with life on the wrong side of the law. I had never been
there myself, but to my surprise, I was not deterred by
it. In fact, it seemed to bring clarity to my thinking and
resolve not to overlook a single detail. After all,
blackmail carried a punishment of 2-15 years in
Florida.

I arose early the next morning, made a double-
espresso, and went for a long walk with my notebook
and pen. When a question or idea occurred to me, good
or bad, I wrote it down. When my idea pool dried up, I
would run for five minutes then pop a piece of hard
candy in my mouth. This seemed to jump-start my
creative juices. Afternoon: lunch, nap, shower, and
walk. I went to bed early that evening, arose well-rested
at six, and started again. By the end of day two, I felt
reasonably sure Chloe would be vulnerable to the type
of proposal I was considering, especially if she lived

alone. Maybe Anthony knew or could find out if she had a husband or partner.

A friend had suggested that I use his summerhouse for a few days so I drove to Vermont early the next morning. By ten o'clock I had taken a dip in the cold lake at the foot of his property, eaten a bowl of cereal, and sat myself down on the warm slats at the end of the dock. I was anxious about how I would initially communicate with Chloe, but my subconscious had been at work. It pointed out that I would be harder to find and, God forbid, to convict, if I left behind no sign that I had ever contacted her. If I could watch Chloe's house for signs of life or for Chloe herself, I would not have to contact her beforehand. This revelation was critical to my overall scheme, and when I left the cabin Sunday night, I had the framework of a good plan in mind.

~ ~ ~

The next time I talked to Anthony he sounded genuinely shook up when I told him that Chloe might have killed her father. He also gave me a copy of an assessment he wrote of the new District Attorney. It was an excellent piece of work and I knew it would help me sound knowledgeable and well connected when I talked to Chloe about her money – and mine. I did not ask Anthony if Chloe lived alone because I did not want him to think I had any interest in rekindling my high school feelings for her. I did ask if Chloe were single or attached. Anthony said he did not know, but would try to find out.

~ ~ ~

The next step was to consult my friend Arturo Lena, whose family, according to rumor, was connected to the Mob. I had never asked him about that, of course. A week after returning from Vermont, I went to Art's house ostensibly to watch a Red Sox game, but really to find out how to obtain some fake drivers' licenses. Art handled this request like Johnny Pesky handled a two-bouncer to third. "Here's a number," he said when he realized *I* wanted the driver's licenses. "Call it when you're ready to go there, not before. When they ask who sent you, the answer is Nicky Silverthorne. Be thorough in explaining to them what you want because they can make a driver's license for one hundred bucks that'll withstand no scrutiny or they'll take some dead guy and give you his whole identity, which will withstand a credit check for a mortgage and more. That will run you a lot more, of course. They will call you back with a price and won't start work until you approve. It's cash only, not negotiable, and it won't be cheap."

"One question," I said. "Are these guys dangerous?"

"Just do what you're told. *Capisci?* Don't ask no questions, don't tell no jokes. These people ain't hired for their sense of humor." The next morning, I called the number Art had given me, mentioned his code name, and took my first step in implementing my plan.

The process by which I obtained my documentation took a month and almost emptied my paltry savings account. Getting to their 'studio' involved walks, subway trips, and a fifteen-minute taxi ride while blindfolded. Once there, a nondescript man took my ten grand for the package of documents that, he promised, would withstand scrutiny. They took pictures of me in my three disguises, and showed me my new briefcase with three secret compartments for my three identities. Finally, an androgynous little person wearing tinted glasses and a hat spent an hour instructing me how to wear my disguises and use the documentation. "Never wear your disguises close to home. Your neighbors know your gait and your posture, which enables them to see right through your wig, glasses, and clothing. To disguise your walk, wrap an ace bandage tightly around your left knee for one disguise; wrap it around your right foot and ankle for a different disguise. Also, I suggest a lockable toilet stall for changing identities and you should wear your disguises for several days before using them for real. As you get used to them, you will realize that you do not stand out while wearing this gear and that most people will pay you less attention while you're wearing a disguise. Buy yourself several different styles of hats and jackets. Put them in an easily accessible place. The colors must be muted. Remember, you're trying to blend in, not attract attention to yourself."

The second step in implementing my plan involved acquiring a good lawyer in the Cayman Islands. I did this by contacting the U.S. Interests Section in the British Embassy in Washington. After frustrating delays, I was given telephone numbers for two "esteemed" law offices. I chose one simply because I liked the sound of his name, Jordan Jarett.

Once in phone contact with him, I asked Mr. Jarett about the talk I was hearing that the islands were under increasing pressure to loosen their bank secrecy agreements. Mr. Jarett assured me there would be many more years of talk before that happens. "They have been too good to all of us and to people like you for us to hurriedly dismantle them down," he said in his cultured Caribbean-British accent. Within three weeks I had opened an account in the name of Bert E. Barnett. There was no fee for opening Mr. Barnett's account, but I put five thousand in it, on the theory that the bank should make at least as much as Mr. Jarett had made for mailing Mr. Barnett some forms and then turning them into the office of the Secretary of State of the Cayman Islands.

Having decided that I would not return to my apartment in Boston, I moved my few belongings to a storage locker and dropped off a check for the pro-rated amount of the month's rent under the super's door with an extra hundred dollars for him. There was nothing in the fridge so I unplugged it, along with all the other appliances, and cancelled my post office box. My final act was to take out the last bag of garbage. With all the loose ends tied off, I set out for Ocala, Florida, over 1200 miles south. It was a long trip, but I vowed to stay under the speed limit all the way. My fake documents were impressive, but I did not want to test them.

~ ~ ~

My first night on the road, I called Anthony from a pay phone in the lobby of my motel. He told me he had learned from a trusted source that Scotty had not had a heart problem. In fact, he had recently had a physical and was as fit as could be. Anthony also reported that Chloe had no significant other at the moment and she lived alone. I thanked Anthony sincerely for what he had done, but then told him it might be best if we not communicate again. I was sure he understood that I was working on something and did not want to incriminate him accidently. His parting comment was, "If you ever need a place to hang out, we have an empty bunkhouse out back.

~ ~ ~

From Boston to Jacksonville, the featureless nature of I-95 requires little of a driver and offers him few diversions. So my mind was available and restless. As I stared out the windshield, it kept asking how I could justify running the risks involved in this operation, and in response I kept trying out different answers to the question. I must say, after all that reflection, I had absolutely no second thoughts about what I was going to do. From my perspective, Chloe was a rich psychopath who had murdered my friend – her father – and had tried to injure or perhaps kill me. I figured she had it coming.

The miles clicked by and after twenty-four hours of driving and one six-hour stop in a motel I rolled into Jacksonville. There I turned in my Avis car because I was going to be in Chloe's neighborhood for the next few days and I figured a car with Florida plates would be less conspicuous than one with Massachusetts plates. Details are important.

For the same reason, I wanted to use my most effective disguise, the one with the mustache and glasses. As I was contemplating these tactical matters and walking to the Hertz office to pick up my new car,

I spotted a McDonald's. It was crowded with midday customers so it seemed unlikely that anyone would pay me enough attention to notice that I had entered the men's room clean shaven and exited with a jaunty, greying mustache and a new pair of tinted glasses. By four o'clock, fortified by a cheeseburger and two coffees, I was driving south to Ocala, a different man in a new car with Florida tags and a sharp, Atlanta Braves baseball cap.

I rolled into Ocala at seven in the evening and cruised through the neighborhoods. The smell of money was everywhere. It seemed that each park and yard was manicured and the entire town was sheltered and beautified by flamboyant tropical trees: acacia, live oaks, draped with languid Spanish moss, numerous species of palm, scarlet and yellow blooming poinsettia, schefflera, and others. Ocala was also known for the number of its thoroughbred horse farms and its most famous native son, Early Arrival, won the Triple Crown in 1974. Despite the beauty all around me, I was anxious to find my way to Chloe's house, but I forced myself to wait for darkness.

Her home was located on an enchanting street lined with date palms and festooned with crimson blooming bougainvillea. There was almost no traffic at that time of evening and there were no streetlights. The road to her house was straight, which meant I could keep an eye on comings and goings without using binoculars. Generally speaking, the location was favorable to me. My concern was that police cruisers or a private security company might regularly patrol the street. I would have to leave if they passed my parking area more than twice. After two drive-bys of her house, I headed out of town for the night. I was operating under an old principle: 'if something can go wrong, it will.'" That is why I spent the night in Gainesville, a full twenty miles north of Ocala.

At 6:15 the next morning, wearing my new disguise, I pulled into an ideal parking place. It was within sight of Chloe's house and between two cars whose owners were probably playing tennis down the hill. Twelve hours later, as the heat and humidity of central Florida began to ease slightly, Chloe appeared in her driveway, stretched briefly, and took off running down the sidewalk – directly at me. It scared the hell out of me and the only response I managed was to flip down my sun visor, which partially blocked her view of my face. Despite that, we saw each other from a distance of only six feet. I was sure she did not recognize me, though. Darkness was falling and I had on my full disguise, mustache, wig, and hat. She disappeared into the fading light and I considered making my move when she returned, but my hands were still shaking and my heart, still pounding from the shock of seeing her running right at me.

I repositioned the car and waited for her return. In the absence of street lamps and under two enormous banyan trees, twilight quickly faded to pitch darkness. Thirty minutes later, Chloe reappeared running strongly up the hill towards her home. I watched her carefully with the binoculars as she bounced up the stairs and pulled open her front door. Her family had never locked either the ranch house or their town home. I was happy to see Chloe had brought that custom with her to her new house.

Hanging around until she returned was smart. I knew that most serious runners – and Chloe was one – adhere faithfully to their routines. I was so sure Chloe would run for about thirty minutes the next day starting around sunset that I took the day off. This not only reduced the time I was exposed on her street, but also allowed me to sleep late, go over what I was going to say to her one last time, and make sure my small satchel had the crucial items I would need when I entered the house. I had a leisurely lunch, took a nap and a shower and began my vigil at five o'clock in the evening.

Chloe left her house in her running togs at 6:35. At 6:40, after pulling on a pair of surgical gloves, I entered the house by a back door. Assuming Chloe would enter the house using the same door she used when she left, I studied the entry area to figure how I could best use the element of surprise to subdue her quickly and quietly. After looking around the basement, I decided a small utility room would be the best place to take her because there was no window or door leading to the outside. I went to the kitchen next, pulled a left-handed cotton glove from my satchel and slid it over the surgical glove on my left hand. Lastly, I took from my satchel a squirt gun, pointed it at the kitchen sink and pulled the trigger. It worked perfectly. After washing the sink, there was nothing to do but wait. Squirt gun in hand, I stood on the other side of the living room from the large bay window and waited to see my old girlfriend walk across her front lawn, up the steps and into my arms. My heart was pounding.

Just as Chloe opened her front door, I pumped the last squirt of chloroform into the cotton glove on my left hand. She probably never smelled its sweet scent. As she took her second step beyond me I slammed into her from behind, wrapping my right arm around both her arms at elbow-level and locking the chloroform-soaked glove over her nose and mouth. I drove her hard into the living room carpet and felt her struggle with great strength to throw me off her back. But she fought only briefly. I felt the tension drain from her muscles before she went limp. I pulled a roll of duct tape out of my satchel and took several wraps around her ankles, added a few more around her wrists, and finally I secured several big strips over her mouth. Convinced she would be going nowhere and making no noise, I put each article back in the satchel: tape, squirt gun, and cotton glove. I kept my surgical gloves on but removed my wig, mustache, and glasses and placed them in the satchel too. I wanted her to see me. I was not sure how the chloroform would affect her mind and it certainly would not do to have her think she had been hallucinating. Two minutes had passed and she was beginning to regain her senses. This relieved me. Had she remained unconscious for five minutes or more she could have suffered lasting brain damage from the chloroform. I picked her up, carried her downstairs and into the utility room. There I sat her upright on the sofa.

When she first opened her eyes they did not focus. She was half-conscious; she shook her feet, arms and legs, and a muffled sound found its way through the tape. Then her eyes widened in terror and she shook even harder. I placed my hand on her shoulder and said, "Relax, I promise I am not going to hurt you." I gave her a few seconds to process this information and continued. "Do you know who I am?"

Chloe nodded. "Is my name Frank?" She shook her head, keeping her frightened eyes on me. "Is it Remington?" She shook her head again. "Is it Sandor?" A nod. I held my hands in front of her. "Nod your head one time for each finger you see. She nodded seven times. "Good," I said. "Now, listen carefully. I want to repeat: I am not going to hurt you. If you cooperate, this will be over in fifteen minutes. Do you understand?" Nod.

She sat bolt upright, all senses working. I could tell. I pulled up a folding chair and sat leaning forward looking directly at her. "The grand jury is going to consider your case soon," I began, "but they don't hold the keys to your future. I do. Let me explain. District Attorney Andrew Snyder isn't a big fan of Scotty. The other day in private he said, 'Leave Scotty alone. He's finally quiet and I'd like him to stay that way.' Also, Snyder's new to the job and probably doesn't want to start off with such a controversial case. So, I'm quite sure that if a grand jury voted tomorrow, you would not be indicted."

"But, Chloe, I know you killed your father, just like you almost killed me back in high school. I know your relationship with him was a disaster and I know you goaded him into racing you on horseback the morning he died. I'm also pretty sure the rumors about his heart

94

were not true. Is that right?" Chloe nodded and I silently thanked Anthony. Admitting the rumors were false was close to admitting she killed him. I pushed on. "Did you have something special planned for that ride? Yes, of course you did. You had everything arranged to make your murder plan look like a lovely morning ride. Your friend Gladys was with you so she could testify about how helpful and solicitous you were with your father all morning, but she knew nothing of the killing moment, did she? She did not see Lucky's crazed bucking and spinning, or Scotty's violent, awkward death because she had been left in the dust when the race started, right?

"So, the question is: how did you make Lucky buck him off remotely? I bet you asked someone. I know I did. I called the Hot Shot prod factory in Lincoln, Nebraska, and asked if they had such a thing as a remote control prod. The man said, 'We don't sell 'em, but you can make 'em in about ten minutes. Just buy you a remote control garage door opener and take out the starter button, the antenna, and the switch. Solder two wires from the business end of the prod to two flat pieces of metal and tape those metal plates to the rump of the cattle that don't move fast enough. That'll speed 'em up all right.'" I stopped talking like the man at the factory at that point because I wanted Chloe to remember everything I said. The more she remembered, the more likely she was to do what I wanted her to do.

I waited, then changed back to myself. "All you had to do, Chloe, was hide the prod, which is the size of a pen, and the receiver and switch, each the size of a pack of cigarettes, in Lucky's saddlebag and place the metal pieces so they lay flat against the horse when you tied the saddlebag down. When the race started you waited until Gladys had fallen way behind and you and Scotty were galloping at full speed. Then you pushed the button and WHAM, 4500 volts hit your father's horse in the rump! That's a lot of juice, man. Not enough to kill the horse, but it would certainly make her buck like the baddest goddamned bronco in Florida as long as you held that button down. Your poor dad flew off that horse, did a half-flip and landed on his head. It snapped his neck and killed him instantly. And that's what's called cold-blooded, premeditated patricide."

After the 'accident,' you just took the parts out of the saddlebag quick and easy and stashed them away until you were safe and alone and could dispose of them permanently." I stopped my monologue and looked at Chloe. Her eyes were cast downward.

"Do I have your attention now?" I asked Chloe. She looked up, but did not nod this time. "Well, if I have *your* attention, imagine how interested the DA would be if he were here.

"Was that pretty close to how it happened?" I asked. "If so, there might be a small patch or two of burnt hair or a bald spot where the voltage entered Lucky's body. The genius in this story is, even if I've got some of its elements wrong, it's so feasible that any grand jury would want to indict you. And if they found you guilty of murder, they'd still be doing the right thing, they'd just be doing it for the wrong reasons. And the last fun part is, Florida uses the electric chair. How ironic!

"It's a strong case, no doubt, but your greed makes indictment a certainty. You had a twenty million dollar windfall waiting for you when Scotty died, but you had to have it right away and were willing to kill your own father to get your hands on it.

"Chloe, are you listening to me?" Again she nodded. I have put everything I have just told you, and more, on paper. All of it is in this manila envelope which will be delivered to DA Snyder on Wednesday morning, but you have the power to stop that from happening. Do you want to know how?" Another nod.

I laid a deposit slip from my Cayman bank on the table next to her and said, "By depositing one million dollars into this bank account before the close of business next Tuesday. Let me stress, you must make the deposit anonymously and to the numbered account. No names are to be mentioned. I will call the bank at close of business Wednesday. If the entire million has been deposited, I will burn this envelope and say nothing more about it to anyone ever. I know you are thinking, 'He'll be back in a year asking for more.' But I won't. Part of the reason I need this money is because my mother is ill and has no insurance. I swear to you on her name that I will not ask you for money again.

"One last thing now. I want you to slide off the sofa and make your way to the stairs and then to the upper floor. I want to be sure you can make it to the kitchen counter where I left you a pair of scissors. Chloe made it easily enough up the stairs and into the kitchen. Once there, I ordered her to go back to the room and wait for thirty minutes before leaving it.

I had parked in a cull-de-sac two blocks from Chloe's house. I tried to walk casually through the very dark night with satchel in hand. I turned in my rental car at the Jacksonville airport at 9:10 and was asleep in my hotel in New York by 2:00 a.m.

EPILOGUE

Chloe deposited one million dollars in Mr. Barnett's account before the deadline I had given her. I kept my word and did not make contact with District Attorney Snyder. He followed his political instincts and saw to it that the grand jury did not indict Chloe for the death of her father.

After helping my mother select a new apartment, I placed my money in several Caribbean banks, and moved to a small town in Panama under another assumed name. I lived a comfortable but solitary life there with seven geese I kept in my fenced yard as an alarm in case of an intruder. I kept my escape plan current and never went anywhere without two handguns, one in my shoulder holster, one on my ankle. I chose the solitary life because I knew Chloe would use her money to look for me and to take me down if she found me. After eighteen months in Panama, I moved to a gated community on Grand Cayman Island.

Although I planned to stay there forever, I began to miss home. I had enjoyed week after week, month after month of perfect sun, sand, and the turquoise sea, but I dreamed of Boston delis, fall football, a couple of friends, and my mother, whom I had not seen in over five years. So I returned to the States and rented a small house on the grounds of an estate in Newport, Rhode Island. It met my needs perfectly. I received my mail at the owners' address. I parked my car in a shed behind the house, and I even put up a fence and bought seven new geese.

On the morning of my forty-fourth birthday, I awoke with a pounding headache. I rolled out of bed and stumbled into the bathroom to find some aspirin. There I was greeted by seven headless geese and a note written on the mirror that said,

Happy Birthday
B seein U

8

Fowl Play

Robert Coburn

Valentine had never realized he was a chicken. He had been a pet from the day he'd hatched – which was on Valentine's Day – and had always thought he was just another human being who had the run of the house. But when he became a grown rooster, he had been put on his own.

It was a confusing time for him. Not to mention the identity crisis.

He'd been scratching around behind a restaurant off Duval Street when a young rooster approached.

"I'm Charlie Chaplin," the bird clucked.

"Hi, I'm Valentine."

Charlie Chaplin crowed.

"But you're a rooster!" he cackled. Then leveling a suspicious eye, added, "How'd you get that name?"

"From the people I used to live with."

"That won't work for you. How about Rudy Valentino?"

"Why?"

Charlie Chaplin crowed again and flapped his wings.

"Duh, because all Key West chickens have movie star names."

Valentine had no idea what he was talking about. Movie star names? He wished he could go back home.

"Why is that?" he clucked. "Why do Key West chickens have movie star names?"

"Why?" Charlie Chaplin clucked back and raised his hackles. "You might as well ask why did the chicken cross the road, you silly bird."

Valentine thought it odd to have asked a sensible question only to have a more difficult one thrown back at him. He wondered if this cocky little fellow knew the answer to anything. He'd try one more.

"Are there enough movie star names for everyone?" he clucked.

"We recycle."

Valentine decided he'd better go along if he was going to get along.

"Okay, I'm Rudy Valentino. Thanks, Charlie."

"That's *Charlie Chaplin*, if you please. Key West chickens always go by their full name. It's the protocol."

Right then the back door to the restaurant's kitchen banged open and a man shooed them away with a shout and a wave of hands.

"The same to you!" Charlie Chaplin squawked back at him as they hightailed it.

"Where to now?" Rudy Valentino clucked after they'd taken refuge in some bushes.

Charlie Chaplin thought for a moment.

"House behind that fence up ahead has cats," he clucked with a glint in his eye. "Probably got a full bowl of food. You hungry?"

The two roosters flew up to the top of the fence. Rudy Valentino was pleased with how easily he'd made the short hop. He'd never spent much time learning the rudiments of flight. Guessed he was a natural. But he was surprised to see two large cats staring up at him from the deck below.

"What about those things?" he clucked in alarm.

"Cats are nothing," Charlie Chaplin clucked. "Watch out for dogs, though."

With that he hopped off the fence and trotted straight for the food bowl. The cats skedaddled. Rudy Valentino cackled and joined him.

"You have a roost?" Charley Chaplin clucked between pecks, the bowl quickly emptying.

"Nothing permanent."

"You can bunk with me, if you like."

Rudy Valentino thought that was an excellent idea and they left the cats' yard.

"My place is down the lane," Charlie Chaplin clucked.

They were on Duval Street, having passed Bogart's Irish Bar and coming up to Whalton Lane.

"The people back there also put out cat food," he added with a sly wink.

The roost was under an overhang on a shed.

"Wow, who's that?" Rudy Valentino cackled, spotting a rooster sporting flashy plumage standing on the sidewalk across from them. A plump and striking-looking hen was with him.

"George Raft," Charlie Chaplin clucked under his breath and averted his eyes. "He's one tough bird. Hangs out with James Cagney."

"She's nice," Rudy Valentino clucked. "What's her name?"

"Bette Davis and don't even think about crossing that road."

~~~

Several blocks over on Margaret Street, Greta Garbo had lingered longer than she should've, mooching treats from the kitchen at Michael's. Now it was getting dark and she was hurrying along Passover Street to get to her roost on Poorhouse Lane. A snap of something moving in the dark bushes along the street caused her to turn her head. But her neck was wrung before she'd even had a chance to see.

~~~

Rudy Valentino had readied himself for the first welcoming crow of the new day and was about to send forth when Charlie Chaplin flapped a wing for him to stop.

"I wouldn't do that," he clucked quietly.

Rudy Valentino ruffled his hackles.

"Why not? It's almost daylight. I was going to give three."

"It'll screw up our deal here. Last rooster that woke everybody up got himself netted. Keep your beak shut until later."

"How about we go somewhere else?" Rudy Valentino clucked. "I'm feeling kind of anxious. I really need a good crow."

"Hmm, suppose we could."

With the eastern sky fast bluing, they made their way down Olivia Street and toward Simonton, the cock-a-doodle-do telegraph already up and running throughout the island.

"I have to crow right now," Rudy Valentino cackled nervously. "I can't stand it any longer."

Both roosters stopped at the corner and, rearing back, called out in unison before crossing the street. They continued along Olivia, joyously trading crows back and forth, until they came to Elizabeth Street where a number of chickens had gathered and were noisily clucking. Recognizing Jimmy Stewart in the crowd, Charlie Chaplin walked over.

"What's up?" he clucked.

"Greta Garbo had her neck wrung last night," Jimmy Stewart cackled. "Out by the cemetery."

In chicken parlance, *neck wrung* meant any death other than by natural causes.

"Cemetery's iguana territory," Fred Astaire clucked. "Wouldn't catch me in there. Don't trust those devils. They live under the graves. Did you know that?"

"This wasn't the work of an iguana," Jimmy Stewart clucked. "There's been talk of a dog on the loose. That's your prime suspect."

"Did anyone see what happened?" Charlie Chaplin clucked, ruffling his feathers at the thought of a loose dog.

"No, she wanted to be alone," Jimmy Stewart clucked.

"Exactly my point," Fred Astaire cackled. "And look where it got her."

"It must be the times we're living in," Gloria Swanson clucked. "Tyrone Power got fried just the other day."

He'd been pecking at an electrical extension cord that was stuck in the socket.

A murmur of clucks rose from the group. Someone had noticed a tourist across the street pointing a camera at them.

"Smile, everyone," Joan Crawford clucked.

They all cackled at the thought of a chicken smiling. The tourist seemed delighted and snapped several pictures before walking on.

"Seriously, folks," Randolph Scott clucked, flapping his wings to get everyone's attention. "Fred Astaire has brought up an important issue. No one should be alone with a dog on the loose. We need to go in pairs. Four eyes are better than two."

"What about our broods?" Ann Sheridan clucked. "Hard to keep our eyes on them. Little ones are always running around, well, like a..."

"Don't bother saying the rest of it," Humphrey Bogart clucked at her. "We get what you mean. How about this? A rooster accompanies his hen whenever and wherever she goes when she has a brood."

"I don't know about that ..." a few roosters clucked. The hens cackled noisily back at them in admonishment.

"Time we face up to our responsibilities, gentlemen," Jimmy Stewart clucked. "Otherwise, I'm afraid there're going to be more necks wrung."

The next day that ominous warning would become a fact.

~~~

Katharine Hepburn had gotten to her favorite scratching place early. Still, a few ibises had beaten her there and were well into their breakfasts. The children's play park at Poorhouse Lane and William Street offered a rich territory for unearthing insects and worms. She'd been busy attacking an ant colony behind a tree when she had come upon the carnage.

~~~

"Another neck wrung," Joseph Cotton clucked in dismay. "Something has to be done."

He and several other roosters had met on the short stretch of Grinnell Street between Olivia and Truman to discuss the worsening situation.

"Poor Lana Turner," Errol Flynn clucked. "At least, Vivien Leigh was able to take in her brood. Poor little things."

"Has anyone seen this loose dog?" Joseph Cotton clucked. "Wonder what it looks like?"

"Only Greta Garbo and Lana Turner so far," Errol Flynn clucked back sarcastically. "It's a loose dog. What more do you need to know?"

"It must live around here," Joseph Cotton clucked, ignoring the question. "Greta Garbo had her neck wrung on Passover Street and Lana Turner's not far from there."

"Suppose one of us could act as a decoy to draw him out," Errol Flynn clucked thoughtfully. "And when he tries his funny business, the rest of us could chase him away. Throw in a few sharp pecks for good measure."

"The decoy's a good idea but we'll need some muscle for this chicken fight," Joseph Cotton clucked. "I'm getting on the cock-a-doodle telegraph."

"Send for Lee Marvin," Clark Gable cackled.

"He's no spring chicken," Earl Flynn clucked.

"Back him up with George Raft and James Cagney," Clark Gable clucked.

"Now that's something to crow about!" Errol Flynn cackled.

Joseph Cotton crowed three times, each one slightly nuanced. A distant rooster repeated them exactly. And on and on until it'd reached the intended party. That was how the cock-a-doodle telegraph worked. Like a charm.

~~~

Charlie Chaplin and Rudy Valentino had apparently been out of range and hadn't heard any of this, however. Or maybe it was just because they were too tanked at the moment to bother.

They'd earlier come upon a dumpster in an alley behind a bar. Some of the garbage bags inside it were ripped open and their contents had spilled out. This had included a fair amount of rum-soaked cherries and orange slices.

"These red things are delicious!" Rudy Valentino clucked, gobbling up a cherry.

"Try the orange-colored ones," Charlie Chaplin cackled.

"I already have. I like the reds better."

Charlie Chaplin crowed off-key and pecked out another orange slice.

~~~

Lee Marvin and James Cagney had both shown up in a flurry of threatening crows while still on Johnson Lane. Edward G. Robinson had arrived with hardly a cluck. George Raft had been the last to get there.

"This plan stinks!" James Cagney crowed.

"Save the tough-guy act for later," Lee Marvin clucked. "Maybe the dog will appreciate it."

James Cagney raised his hackles, then turned his attention to a bug scurrying past on the ground.

"I like the plan," George Raft clucked, his eyes hooded. "Who's the decoy?"

"I'm the decoy, see?" Edward G. Robinson crowed.

That settled, it was time for action.

"Let's move out!" Lee Marvin crowed.

The small squadron meandered through the cemetery, stopping occasionally to scratch in the freshly mown grass.

"We'll take up our position behind the fence," Lee Marvin clucked quietly as they neared Passover Street.

Suddenly, a ball of fur exploded from behind a tombstone! Edward G. Robinson, who'd been on point, squawked and flapped his wings but it was too late. The dog had him by the tail feathers.

The rest scattered in every direction, running like chickens with their heads ... again.

~~~

Rudy Valentino and Charlie Chaplin, still feeling no pain, strutted up Margaret Street toward the cemetery. Angry barking and frantic cackling greeted them as they entered the grounds.

"Whas' tha' ruckus?" Rudy Valentino clucked.

"Isn' tha' Lee Marvin up there?" Charlie Chaplin clucked.

"Yesh, an' Edward G. Robinson's with him."

A scattering of russet feathers lay on the ground below the headstone.

"Wha' happen to your tail?" Rudy Valentino crowed.

The dog, which had chased after the others without success, now spotted them.

"Look out!" Lee Marvin crowed.

Rudy Valentino did the only thing he could. He crowed but in fright rather than delight. However, due to the effect of the spiked cherries, it came out as a ferocious war cry.

The dog put its tail between its legs and whimpered.

"Do that again," Charlie Chaplin cackled.

Rudy Valentino let forth with another crow, this time even more horrifying.

"Let's get him," Charlie Chaplin cackled.

Both charged with hoarse crows and wings flapping. The terror-stricken dog turned to run but not before Rudy Valentino had given him a sharp peck for good measure.

Lee Marvin and Edward G. Robinson hopped off of the headstone. The latter having some difficulty maintaining balance.

"We showed that dog who's boss!" Lee Marvin crowed.

Rudy Valentino and Charlie Chaplin didn't respond. They were too hungover.

~~~

Back at the roost on Whalton Lane, Rudy Valentino had begun to perk up and was feeling hungry. He hopped on the fence only to see that the cat food bowl had been moved and was now in some kind of cage. However, its door was open. He'd no sooner walked inside that it slammed shut behind him.

~~~

The next day Rudy Valentino was taken to the animal shelter. But it was found that placing a rooster for adoption was a tricky business. There were obstacles that couldn't be overcome. So the people there decided to just let him live with them.

He eventually became a celebrity to all who visited.

The Hollywood End.

9

Savannah Wind

John Guerra

I stepped over the sleeping rooster at the top of the stairs and almost tumbled to the street.

Hazards at every step. In this town, nature is the enemy. The brutal sun. Hurricanes. Malaria. For baby chicks, hawks that strike from nowhere, leaving behind grieving hens to count what's left. The rooster is a survivor of that.

I cursed him anyway and walked under a bright moon toward the waterfront. It was a deep January night, with frangipani layered on the warm breeze, but the fragrance wasn't quite enough to cover the sour odor of beer and horse droppings as I cut through the alleys behind the ale houses.

From beneath a weathered sail hung high above a dark beer garden came a song, sweetly sung by what my ears took to be a young woman. I stopped to listen:

I had a dream the other night, when everything was still; I thought I saw Susanna dear, a comin' down the hill. The buckwheat cake was in her mouth, a tear was in her eye, I says, 'I've coming from the South' – Susanna, don't you cry.

It was a mournful tune for the times.

The Civil War ended a few months ago and the South was broken. Former slaves and the bitter children of Dixie were now wandering the world, looking for a place to begin. Key West was an undamaged place, where ships fleeing the flames of Charleston, Savannah, and other charred harbors resupplied before sailing on to Central and South America. Some men came ashore and hid in the whorehouses along Thomas Street, emerging only after their former crewmembers raised sail and slipped over the southern horizon.

I lingered a few moments in the moonlight of the alley, drawn to the sadness in the singer's voice.

I come from Alabama with my Banjo on my knee – I'm goin' to Louisiana my true love for to see.

I heard shuffling feet and turned.

A drunken figure in a federal Army uniform stumbled past me, slowly making his way in the direction I had come, heading God knows where. His horse, reins dragging, clopped along behind him. The unsteady soldier was probably too drunk to ride.

There were a lot of military men in the Southernmost City. Five of the U.S. Navy's finest warships bobbed in the moonlit anchorage just outside the harbor. A war-beaten ironclad, dented and scarred by cannon fire, lay against the seawall at the Navy yard.

In addition to hundreds of sailors and officers at the Navy Yard, the U.S. Army fort at the entrance to Key West harbor was finally complete. Started in 1831, Fort Zachary Taylor was now home to Company H, 4th U.S. Infantry, as well as 140 of the largest smooth-bore cannon in the Union's possession. That hellish weaponry included some of the best-rifled parrot guns available. Their menacing barrels poked through a line of archways in the fort's brick façade.

Soldiers and sailors are usually everywhere, mingling in the streets and bars with the tradesmen, mercenaries, throw-downs and scoundrels that populate this tiny city. Everyone is armed, short-tempered, and for some odd reason, each thinks himself a comedic actor in the manner of John Wilkes Booth.

The inebriated soldier must have been one of the 400 or so artillery and mounted cavalry barracked at the fort. I watched him turn left from the alley on to Angela Street and sure enough, a minute later, the horse turned the corner, following right behind him. I smiled. A loyal horse is hard to find.

The young singer's voice faded behind garden walls as I walked to the end of the alley and turned left on Eaton Street to the flickering gaslight of Front Street. The cobblestone lane, with its theater house and ship chandleries, runs the length of the waterfront. The street is usually bustling with trade, but at 3 a.m., there is only a group of men with an oil lantern standing in the middle of the street. At their feet is what looks to be a bundle of women's clothes.

This must be the crime scene.

My name is Franklin Dover, a criminal investigator for the Reconstruction Governor of Florida. Under the always-shifting rules of Reconstruction set down by Washington, I'm part detective, part jailer, and wholly underpaid. There's one like me in every county in Florida. We investigate everything from counterfeiting – a big problem since the South collapsed – to stolen cargo, robbery, and of course, murder. The military handles its own.

Stillness inhabits a dead body so thoroughly that the absence of life is apparent a hundred feet away. I knew the woman was gone even before I saw the blood pooled around her head. I nodded to the men standing around her.

Her jacket – of expensive European design - was pulled off one shoulder. Her arms were splayed outward as if she had tried to swim through the cobblestone. Her riding crop was in one of her gloved hands.

The deceased wore a long riding skirt over boots, fashionable with women on horseback who inspected their large holdings before the war took their society away. She was slim and looked to be in her 30s – where her head and face hadn't been beaten.

"It's about time you got here," said a fat man holding the lantern. It was Tubby, my associate, who got paid even less than I did. "I sent Louie for you an hour ago."

"I got your note but I had trouble getting past my rooster," I said, frowning at his rudeness.

"So you got cock-blocked," a man I didn't recognize said to snickers from the other men. See what I mean about comedians?

Tubby shushed them. "They found the victim," he said, gesturing to two men standing next to him. The taller of the two men nodded at me. "This one stayed with the body while the other came and got me in the saloon. These other men walked up after I got here."

I asked, "Anybody see what happened?"

"We was walking back from the Jumping Joker," the taller man said, pointing down the street in the direction of the fort, "and saw her just lying here in the street. She was taking her last breath when we got to her. She was just like you see her now, except her leg was movin' a little."

I studied the other men. They wore sweat-stained shirts and soiled breeches over the sturdy, flat shoes dock workers favor. Under the lantern light their eyes were weary shadows from the day's toil but there was also sadness at seeing a lady taken while so young and so fair.

The sly comment about the rooster had been an attempt to lighten the sting of what lay at our feet.

"Did you men hear anything - anyone yelling, any commotion? No one saw this woman attacked?" I asked again. Their replies took the form of mumblings of no sir, shuffling feet, and shaking heads.

"Clear them out," I said.

Tubby motioned everyone, including the two men who found the dead woman, to the grass on the side of the street. There they stood, their eyes glued to the unfortunate woman. Tubby returned with his lantern and he held it above the lady frozen on the cobblestone.

"So what do you think?" I asked Tubby.

"She's dead."

"I agree. What killed her?" Sometimes you have to urge Tubby along.

"She was thrown from her horse and hit her head on the cobblestone," he said.

"I don't think so, Tub."

I leaned down and pulled the woman's hair, sticky with blood, back from her face. "See how her skull is injured? It's not one blow, but several along the forehead and there's a deep gouge in the temple, too. Someone hit her with a blunt object. Hand me your lantern."

I stepped away from the body and swung the lantern slowly, looking for something. There it was.

"Tub, see the scrape marks on the cobblestone? That's from a startled horse being restrained by an attacker. Someone grabbed the reins and this woman tried to turn the horse to avoid her assailant."

"You're right, Frank," Tubby said. "She tried to back the horse up, then tried to break around the attacker. But the attacker, who either was on foot or on another horse, must have had hold of the bit."

"Check out the riding crop."

My rotund associate leaned forward and put his hands on the ground, then lowered his considerable bulk into a kneeling position. He pulled a magnifying glass from his jacket pocket and lowering his face almost to the ground, trained the glass on the tip of the riding crop. I held the lantern close.

"Nothing there," he said.

"There's no blood on the tip, so she either didn't have time to strike her attacker, or she fought back but didn't make any meaningful blows. Or hit him about the back or chest where clothes hide the stripes. If she hit him in the face, we may link the attacker that way."

I grabbed the victim's shoulder and gently turned her on her back. Tubby helped by grabbing her boots and turning. Her riding jacket was soiled from the fall and torn above the right breast. I saw something glinting in the lantern's light - a thin, silver necklace. I handed Tubby the oil lamp, lifted her head, and removed the chain from around her neck.

The blood was still wet on the chain as I held it up and dangled a silver, heart-shaped locket into my palm. I opened the locket. Inside was a tiny photograph of a Confederate private, his eyes wide and expressionless. The photographer's flash – accomplished by the use of gunpowder – surprises subjects, creating an expression of extreme nervousness.

Some soldiers on both sides of the Mason-Dixon Line believed images taken before going off to war made it more likely that a bouncing cannon ball would find them.

The rebel soldier in the locket looked to be much younger than the woman at my feet. He was 16 if he was a day. I read the salutation aloud: *"To Lily, my beloved sister. Savannah, Ga., 1861"*

Tubby sighed and I looked down at the unfortunate woman in the riding clothes. *Her name was Lily*. Was her brother already waiting for her in the great hereafter? Probably, or she'd have a more recent image of her little brother in that locket. Or maybe he was on crutches, a leg lost to a cannon ball, panhandling in the streets of New Orleans and afraid to come home.

I felt anger under the moonlight. They were still counting, but the U.S. War Department believed more than half a million men on both sides had died in the war - not counting more than a million horses and mules and everything else that was blown apart or died of dysentery.

Now this young lady. Nearly a year after Appomattox, the killing was still going on. You'd think after what we'd just been through that no one would want to harm the hair on anyone else again.

"You recognize her, Tubby? You ever see her before?" I asked my associate.

"Nope. Clearly she's not from Key West. She was a woman of means from a wealthy family, from what I gather. She's got to be from one of the private merchant ships." He pointed to the big sailing vessels and the large coal-burning ship anchored in the moonlit harbor.

"I think you're right. At this late hour, she was probably heading back to a ship – she is on Front Street after all - when she was attacked."

I pointed to a large, three-masted sailing packet that dwarfed the low buildings along the waterfront. "I bet it's that one. But first, we need to get Miss Lily here to a safe place until we can figure out what's going on," I said.

"I already have that taken care of, Frank," Tubby said, looking up Front Street at lantern swinging in the night.

A black man at the reins of a buckboard came clopping up Front Street and pulled back on the reins just short of me, Tubby and Lily's prone remains. An elderly black man, small in stature, sat next to the driver. The buckboard driver pulled back the handbrake and lifted his hat in greeting.

"Hello Frank," said Skinny Green, the director of Greenleaf Mortuary. "As Tubby requested, I've come to take this young lady off the street."

"Hello, Skinny, hello Sammy," I said to Skinny's elderly helper, lifting my hat to both in return. "I thank you. Can you do me a favor and keep the news of this lady's demise from getting out?"

"You can bet on it," Skinny said.

As Tubby and I walked toward the large sailing ship at the docks, I heard him muttering under his breath.

"What is it, Tubs?"

"Where's her horse?"

"Good question, Tubs. If I'm correct about which ship she's from, we'll get an answer to that."

I was right. The ornate wood-carved nameplate on the stern of the 120-foot packet I pointed to read *Savannah Wind*. We walked along the seawall in the shadow of the towering hull to the gangplank, which was down. Looking up, I saw a man leaning against the ship's rail, smoking a pipe. The night's watch.

I yelled up to him: "Halloo, permission to come aboard?"

"Who might you be?" the man asked with a marked southern drawl.

"I am Franklin Dover, and this is my associate, Tubby Simonton. Do you have a few moments to speak with us?"

The pipe smoker stared down at us for a long moment. "About what?"

"We are trying to find someone. Her name is Lily." Tubby turned and stared at me but thankfully kept his mouth shut.

The man straightened, looked left and right, and considered what to do. He leisurely tapped the pipe on the outside of the rail, sending sparks cascading to the water. He came down the plank, using the handrail to steady himself, then stood before us.

The slight man's face showed caution but something else ... concern? He wore a neatly trimmed beard that hadn't gone fully grey, a Greek fisherman's cap, and a semi-uniform that was laundered and neat.

"You must be the captain," I said.

"Captain Robert Wallace, pleased to meet you and I don't think I'll be seeing Savannah Harbor again anytime soon. (He pronounced it any-tahm). Sherman didn't burn us to the ground but he seized ships and cargo for the Union. I refused to work for him under pay or duress. So we've been on the wind ever since."

I liked him. He was a straight-talker, honest enough that he felt no need to be cagey or spin tales. He eyed me suspiciously.

"Unfortunately for me, I'm the criminal investigator for Key West and most of Monroe County," I said, answering his unasked question. "That is, I'm the civilian law, until the state's leaders decide what permanent form law enforcement will take down here. I'm not alone, of course. I've got Tubby here and the entire U.S. Army and Navy which do their own keeping of the peace."

I knew I'd hit a raw nerve when Captain Wallace flinched.

"To hell with the U.S. Army! They maybe won the war, but they can stop kicking every southern businessman like a dog," the captain barked. "I especially didn't like them coming aboard my ship the way they did — after midnight, no less. Three of them came up the ramp, didn't even ask permission to board and entered the wheelhouse before we had a chance to stop them. They asked me to show them the cargo, the safe, my logs, even our sleeping quarters."

"They do that, searching for contraband," Tubby said, helpfully. I elbowed Tubby to shut him up.

"CONTRABAND!" the captain roared. *"The war's over!* They see a nice bottle of bourbon in your sleeping quarters, they claim it as contraband and drink it. They see a pair of nice riding boots, they claim them as contraband. Saw one of 'em wearing my father's VMI ring as he "inspected" my berth. My father gave me that ring when I came of age!"

Virginia Military Institute, the South's version of West Point. I shook my head at the Army's insult to this man. Fleeing his homeland with the remains of his family's belongings, the captain had to suffer soldiers pecking at what was left, including having to bear the sight of seeing a Union soldier wear his father's service ring.

"They ordered my crew off the ship. I asked them on what authority they were on my boat and they said, 'On account that we'll blow your ship out of the water if you don't comply.'"

That wasn't normal. If the Army searches ships for weapons or contraband, they do it with a warrant from a judge advocate, written orders from the provost marshal, and the commander of the boarding party always gets the signature of the captain whose ship they board. Soldiers don't go rampaging through a boat; the senior officer in the boarding party walks with the captain and keeps things calm, official. With respect. Otherwise, guns get pulled, people get shot. Messy business.

The aggrieved captain realized that Tubby and I weren't the problem and took a deep breath. "Lily left in a hurry," he said worriedly. "The soldiers so upset her that she went below, put the saddle on Snapper – that's her roan - and rode off to get away from them. Union soldiers have a history of mistreating our women in ways that ruin them forever."

Surprised, I asked, "You have stalls down below?"

"Not a stall, really. Lily talked me into bringing her horse so we made a space with hay and a tie-up. When they came aboard, she ran below, dropped the door on the side of the hull – it turns into a ramp - and rode off to avoid the soldiers. She's been gone for a couple of hours but she's a smart gal. She's been through a war and will stay out of sight.

I made the next statement carefully as the captain awaited my reaction.

"So you ran spies."

He looked down, then back at me, holding my gaze. "It was a war, sir, and I did what I could to help the Southern cause."

I nodded, reached into my jacket and pulled out my calling card. "Please tell your daughter that we'd like to help you both recover what was lost to the soldiers tonight."

Captain Wallace nodded grimly and shook my hand. "If you'll excuse me, I'll go back up top and continue watching for my daughter's return." With that, he walked back up the gangplank.

On the walk back to Front Street, Tubby was mumbling again.

"What is it, Tubby?"

"What was all that talk about spies?"

"It was a way of moving rebel spies and their horses. You cut a door in the side of a ship so a horse and rider could quickly exit onto a dock or landing. They could disembark behind Union lines, beat armies to the crossroads, courier secret messages to places no one expected, what have you. Tonight it served Lily, though apparently it was not enough to prevent her death."

"And how cruel, you did not tell a father of his daughter's death! Why not?"

"He'll learn about it soon enough my porcine friend," I answered. "What would he do upon learning his daughter, the last of what he holds precious, has been taken away from him? He'd restart the Civil War right here in Key West, one Yankee at a time. We don't have much time to solve this murder."

"Well," Tubby said, "We're the authorities and it's our job to find justice for the father of poor Miss Lily Wallace."

"Couldn't have said it better, my trusty associate," I said, condescendingly.

Skinny had removed the victim and was gone by the time Tubby and I walked back to the crime scene. Standing above the dried blood in the middle of Front Street, I looked back across the distance to the *Savannah Wind*. The captain could not have seen his daughter murdered from his post at the ship's rail. A copse of tall trees near the street had blocked his view.

"Let's go over to the Jumping Joker and get some breakfast, Tubs. We'll figure out our next move from there."

Night was lifting as we sat quietly digesting our breakfast at a long wooden table inside the Jumping Joker. A cavalry officer on a foaming Army mount pulled up outside and quickly dismounted. Unshaven like most of his fellow cavalry and wearing an unkempt uniform, he walked up to our table. He did not salute, ignoring the usual courtesy the Army gives civilian law enforcement.

"Inspector Dover, Major Stanley Bradley would like to talk to you at the parade ground," he said gruffly without looking me in the eyes.

"Tell him we'll walk over as soon as we're finished here," I told him. He hesitated a moment, and said, "He said for you to come now."

"You tell the major that I'll get there when I arrive there."

With that, the soldier got on his horse and rode back toward the fort.

"This is fortuitous, Tubby," I said, watching the rider disappear up the street. "I can't imagine the major has so quickly heard about our conversation with Captain Wallace. I knew we would need to visit the fort, but not so soon. Let's keep our counsel and not give away anything, hear me?"

"I do, I do," my well-fed friend replied.

~ ~ ~

The sun broke above the sea as we made our way to Fort Zachary Taylor at the mouth of Key West Harbor. The Tub and I were tired, but masterful in intent as we walked past the tropical plants and flowerbeds in the yards of the well-to-do along Southard Street. Insects warmed their wings and began their work among bougainvillea, peonies and starwort.

Then the cobblestone turned into a dirt field on the backside of the fort where Army mules, canvas tents and horse-drawn caissons were parked in no particular order.

In the sunlight grass just below the fort's back wall, a handful of horses flicked their tails and tossed their heads as cavalry attendants washed and rinsed their charges.

Fort Zachary Taylor is a trapezoid, with cannon poking out from gun ports inside the walls and parrot guns on the top of each of four parapets. The army likes 360 degrees of firepower but I swear it makes me uneasy that they still have some of those parrot guns pointed inland at the city's inhabitants. This Southernmost City remained happily under Union control during the entire war. Nevertheless, some of the guns still stare at downtown.

Only Fort Jefferson in the Dry Tortugas is more menacing. Heavily cannoned to guard the approaches to the Mississippi River, Fort Jeff is also a prison for Union Army deserters and a few Confederate officers. Some will be there for life. That doctor is there, too, the one who was in on the assassination of the president. A friend of mine who works on the ship that runs supplies to Fort Jefferson told me they may have the beginnings of a yellow fever epidemic out there.

We entered the back gate and walked across the wide parade ground toward a bear-sized officer sitting in the shade of a big tree. He sat at a small writing desk, making notes in a ledger with a quill pen. The fort's high brick ramparts ran the entire length of the parade ground and wrapped all the way back to the rear wall, like a coliseum. Looking past the major, I could see a line of cannon that ran from one end of the ramparts to the other.

Each cannon pointed through a square of daylight in the fort's façade, ready to rain hell on the sea and the harbor not a quarter mile away.

The major, who had a bull neck and a shock of dark hair under his Union cap, looked up when he heard our footsteps. He quickly closed the book before we got within 20 paces of him and lay the pen down on the desk. He stood up, unfolding like a mountain gorilla rising to meet a foe. His arms were so big the sleeves of his uniform looked ready to split. He had to be 7 feet tall.

"What took you so long, Dover?"

"I had to digest my breakfast major," I said cheerfully. "A man's got to have time after he eats to settle things. I imagine it takes you some time to digest all those bananas you eat." I didn't really say that last thing, but I thought it.

Tubs looked up at the major, wondering where he might run should things go south. And you couldn't go much further south without a boat.

"You solve murder cases?"

"Among other things."

"Anybody get killed last night?" he asked without missing a beat.

I thought carefully. I trusted Skinny to have kept things quiet. "Nope," I said, slowly shaking my head. "Nothing."

"I had a man run a specific errand last night and he hasn't returned. He's a sober man and always does what I ask. I wonder if you could confirm his fate."

"His fate?"

"I sent a rider out looking for him and he came back with the news that a man had been found beaten to death this morning. I think it may be my man."

Things were turning south and interesting at the same time. I would have heard about such a killing. I'm the law. But I had been busy. "What's his name? I'll see what I can find out."

"Private Thad Cochran," the major said. "You'll know him if you find him. A strong, young buck with red hair. His nickname is Private Red."

"All I can do is see if I run into him in the performance of my own duties, major. But I'll do my best."

"Thank you," the giant said. My hand disappeared into his paw as he shook it.

Tubby and I backed away, keeping him in our sights, until we were a hundred feet away. Then we turned and walked out of the fort.

~ ~ ~

The answers came quickly once we neared the Jumping Joker on Front Street. The errand boy was talking to a little flower girl in front of the Joker when he saw us approaching. He was only 11, but I envied this Bahamian youngster for all the tips he made fetching groceries and people.

"Mr. Dover! Mr. Dover!" Louie yelled, running at us on bare feet. "Skinny wanted me to find you. They found a man in an alley off Whitehead Street this morning. He's dead as a doornail."

"Thank you, Louie," I said, smiling down on him. "I hope you don't mind, I don't have any coin to tip you with now. But please run and tell Skinny we are on the way."

Little Louie looked up at me for a long moment. "You already owe me a lot, Mr. Dover."

"I know, I know, Louie. Consider this a public service."

Tubby gave me a shameful look. "You're going to Hell, Frank."

Tubby and I reached the Greenleaf Mortuary, a well-kept, three-story house on Whitehead Street. We stepped from the sunlight into the cool, dark foyer of the funeral home. You don't yell in funeral homes, so I peeked into a backroom where I found Skinny and his assistant standing over a table. On the table lay the still form of a redheaded man in an Army private's uniform.

"About time you got here, Mr. Dover," Skinny said in greeting. *Why does everyone act like I don't come when called?*

I approached the table and stood next to Skinny. "Private Red."

"You already know who this is?" Skinny said, amazed.

"I just spoke with his commanding officer. He told me he was missing."

I took in the damage. "Tubbs, does this look familiar? This man was found in the alley, his head beaten in, just like the young lady Skinny here picked up from Front Street. The only difference is this man's face is nearly gone. Now who is running around Key West, beating people in the head and leaving them to die in the streets?"

Tubby thought a moment. "It has to be the same killer, Frank. It has to be."

"Skinny, who found this victim?"

"The young lady who sings at the Long Lizard, Frank. She lives a couple of blocks from here. She sent Louie for me after she found the body." *That's more money for Louie. He's getting rich.*

~ ~ ~

Tubbs and I nearly ran to the address Skinny gave me. It was an attractive, two-story house only three blocks away. We walked up to the porch and knocked on the door. The door swung open, revealing a young woman of pleasant countenance.

"Miss, I am Frank Dover, an investigator. I understand you found a man in the alley behind this house this morning?"

She smiled sadly and nodded. She was elegant, with her hair piled high and stray locks cascading over her shoulders. She was dressed nicely and was more ladylike than any bar singer I had ever met. She must have been the one whose voice had captured my imagination in the alley.

Then I remembered: The soldier! The drunk soldier followed by the horse!

Brightening, I asked: "I wonder if you could show us where you found the soldier this morning?"

"Of course." She beckoned us in, and we followed her through the front room, through the kitchen and to the back door. We descended plain wooden steps to the back gate. She opened it and we stepped into the alley.

"There, against the fence on the other side of the alley."

Tubs and I walked over to the spot and looked down. There was enough blood and tissue to indicate a mortal wound, that's for sure. I turned to face the woman, who remained just outside her gate. She didn't want to come any closer.

"Young lady, was there a horse? Did you see a horse?" I asked. Tubby shot me a quizzical look.

"Well yes, there was," she said, causing my heart to quicken. "It was over there, nuzzling a saddle bag. It was trying to eat it." She pointed 100 feet down the alley

"Can you describe the horse?"

"It was a beautiful horse, a roan, but not a large horse," she said. "It was healthy, I noted how well kept it was. It was odd, the saddle I mean. It wasn't an Army saddle. It was a fine lady's saddle, expensive."

"Where is the horse now?" I asked.

"The funeral director tied the horse to the back of his buckboard when he came to take the poor man away."

I'm an idiot. "Thank you, young lady, you have a beautiful singing voice."

With that, I and a properly confused Tubby headed back to Greenleaf Mortuary.

"We have our answers, dear friend," I told Tubby as we hustled up the alley and back to Skinny's place.

"Skinny!" I yelled once inside the funeral home. He and his assistant were still in the back room tending to the soldier. "Show me the horse and the saddlebag."

~ ~ ~

Tubby and I crossed the parade ground of Fort Zachary Taylor. The giant major was still at the table under the awning, writing in the same ledger as before.

"Dover!" he yelled in greeting. I hope you have some news for me."

He must have seen the look on my face and knew I had him. As I drew near, he stood to his full height and punched me in the chest as hard as he could. I fell back on my ass. Tubby took a defensive stance.

"And what are you going to do, my fat friend?" the major said as he advanced on my associate.

"You stay where you are," Tubby said, raising his arms like one of those English pugilists.

I grabbed a handful of earth and struggled to my feet, fighting to breathe. I stepped forward to fling dirt and gravel into the major's face. He sidestepped me and hit me with a hammer jab to the chest again. I stumbled back a step but didn't fall. I yanked a Colt Army Model 1860 pistol from beneath my jacket and pulled the hammer back with my thumb. The gorilla froze as I pointed the barrel at his face.

"That's right, you stinking army mule, take another step and I'll blow your head off your simian shoulders," I snarled. "What are you writing in that book?"

I heard a shout and turned. Three soldiers were right behind me, pointing their Springfield Model 1861 rifles at the back of my head. This latest Army rifle used a .58-caliber ball that could easily separate my head from my own shaking shoulders.

Another yell: "What the hell is going on?" It was Col. William H. French, the commander of the fort. He must have been inspecting the artillery under the ramparts, for he had stepped out from under the shadowy arches of the wall.

"This man attacked me," I said. "I am a duly sworn law officer of the Reconstruction Governor of Florida. I believe this man is responsible for the deaths of an innocent woman and a fellow soldier."

The gorilla's face turned white as he stammered something unintelligible.

Col. French ordered his men to lower their rifles. I put my Colt back in my waistband.

"Sit down, Stan," the colonel told the shocked major. "I want to hear this man out. Please, continue, sworn law officer of the Reconstruction Governor of Florida."

I began, hoping I had all my ducks in a row.

"My name is Frank Dover and I was called to the scene of a murder around 3 a.m. this morning. The victim, a young woman, had been beaten in the head probably while she was still on her horse but certainly after she had fallen onto Front Street from her mount. Someone had attacked her as she was returning to the *Savannah Wind*, that large packet you now see in the distance through the cannon port.

"I spoke to her father, Captain Robert Wallace, who owns the *Savannah Wind*. He told me three Army soldiers boarded his vessel without permission - or a warrant - just after midnight. They riffled through the ship's safe, the vessel's cargo, and the family's personal belongings. They confiscated his valuables, claiming them to be war contraband."

I heard the colonel curse under his breath. The major's worried expression told me I was on the right track.

"His daughter, Miss Lily Wallace, fled the ship with what valuables she could quickly pack in her saddle bag. She quickly put a saddle on her horse and rode out a door in the side of the hull. It doubles as a ramp and was used by spies on horseback during the war."

I looked over at Col. French and he nodded at me. The Union must have used the same trick for their spies. "Her father told me she probably rode to a church where she could remain out of view until the soldiers had gone."

"Can you prove this, *Reconstruction law man*?" the major barked. He tried to stand up from the desk.

"Sit down, major! Let the man continue." God bless Colonel French.

"An hour or longer after the soldiers left, Miss Wallace rode up Front Street to return to the *Savannah Wind,* at what must have been around 2 a.m. or so. Private Red was waiting for her, probably in a stand of nearby trees. He surprised her by grabbing the reins of her horse and trying to pull her off, which should have been easy, since she was probably riding side saddle.

She whipped Private Red with her riding crop, but Private Red resorted to force, using the butt of his pistol to beat her to death after she fell from her horse. He put the pistol back in his holster and threw her saddle bag over his shoulder. As he did so, the horse turned and kicked him in the forehead. It knocked him senseless, but that didn't stop him from ripping an expensive brooch from her riding jacket before he left the scene."

I turned to Tubby. "That was the tear in the jacket over her right breast." He nodded.

"This is rubbish, colonel! He doesn't know what he's talking about," the major objected. "Besides, I know Red. He would never do that!"

"Let him continue," the colonel said again, his anger rising.

"Unless he had orders," I said, pointing to the major. "You told me you sent Private Red on an errand last night and that he hadn't returned. I'm guessing he saw Miss Wallace escape the ship with her saddle bag and told you about it after they returned to the fort.

Then you ordered the private back into the streets to find Miss Wallace and get that saddlebag. You suspected that valuables that fit in a lady's saddlebag must be jewelry, expensive jewelry. Again, the stolen broach indicates the nature of the mission you sent him on. To get the rest of the loot, as it were."

"Now, goddammit colonel, don't listen to this man! I would never ..."

I took my shot. "What have you been writing in that book, major? It's got to be important, because you close it every time anyone comes near."

He stammered. "It's ... it's ... Army business ... "

"Which means I can read it." The colonel walked over to the table and motioned to the major to give him the ledger. The major started to stand but reconsidered when the trio of soldiers raised their Springfield rifles at him.

The colonel opened the ledger. He read it for a moment, frowned, and handed it to me. There on the page, was:

Savannah Wind, slip 10. Cannon port 3

There was Private Red's name, and the names of the other two soldiers who had robbed Captain Wallace.

There was a list of "contraband" the men had taken:

Three bolts of silk fabric

Two cases of bourbon

One case of sour mash whiskey

Three hunting shotguns

One military ring (VMI ring: Virginia Military Institute. Captain Wallace's father's class ring.)

$5,000 Confederate (Useless, but the major might not be smart enough to know that).
$15,000 U.S. (Jackpot)

As I read the list, the colonel motioned to an officer across the parade ground. The big major's posture deflated at the sight of the colonel's gesture. He was getting the picture.

I flipped the ledger's pages. Page after page memorializing illegal Army "raids for contraband" ordered by the now-cornered officer.

"You got quite a haul going on here, major," I said, slamming the ledger shut. "Why would you ask for my help if you knew I might find out what you were up to?"

"I expected you to just find out who killed Private Red and leave it at that. I had no idea a young lady had been killed." I can't believe it. I hear remorse, just a little, in the gorilla's voice.

That's because a soldier carrying wrist and ankle chains is crossing the lawn toward our little party. Those would be for the major.

"I have more unfortunate news, colonel," I said to the major's boss. "The major here has been using your fort to threaten and rob Southern ship owners at gunpoint."

The colonel's eyebrows arched. I opened the ledger again to the *Savannah Wind* page.

"See that line in the ledger that says, 'Slip 10, cannon 3?' At first glance it didn't mean much to me either, until I remembered your men threatened to blow Captain Wallace's ship out of the water if he resisted their attempts to rob him. *The Savannah Wind* was moored in Slip 10."

The colonel turned to look at Cannon Number 3, just inside the wall. It was pointed toward the large packet, clearly visible along the seawall at Slip 10. The horror dawned him and I saw the colonel's fists clench and his face turn red with rage.

"You trained U.S. Army cannon on civilian ships, while they lay under *our protection in Key West Harbor!*" The colonel shouted into the major's face. "You will be hanged for this one."

The major lowered his head and stared at the top of the desk. I love military justice.

"What then of the private? Who killed Private Cochran?" Col. French asked, using the late private's proper name out of respect.

"I watched the killer stalk Private Cochran," I confessed to a shocked Army. By now we were surrounded by dozens of curious soldiers of all ranks and disposition. I stood in the middle of the crowd, choosing my words carefully. Tubbs was standing next to me, but he was being very quiet. In fact, after I said this, he took three steps away from me.

"Let me explain. I was on my way to Miss Lily's crime scene when I heard a woman's voice singing from a garden bar. I was in the alley, out of view, when a soldier, who I took to be inebriated, stumbled past me in the alley.

"A horse – which I took to be his horse – trailed behind him by about 30 paces, its reins dragging in the dirt of the alley. When the major told me this morning that Thad – Private Cochran - was a sober, nondrinking man, I realized that the man I took to be too drunk to ride had in fact, suffered a head injury. A kick from a horse. A kick delivered while the private was killing Miss Wallace and stealing her valuables.

"After he put the sapphire broach he ripped off Miss Wallace's jacket into the saddle bag, he tried to escape by way of the alleys. With his skull fractured and his wits half gone, he either did not realize that Miss Wallace's horse was following him or he wasn't steady enough to break into a run. I watched him walk around a corner and out of sight and by God, that horse followed him around that same corner.

"Then, about an hour ago, I met with the woman who found Private Cochran's body. She recounted how she was just getting home from her night job – about 4 a.m. – when she came upon a horse nuzzling a saddlebag in the alley behind her house on Petronia Street. Nearby was Private Cochran, dead on the ground where Miss Wallace's horse had finished him off.

"Skinny, the funeral director, had picked up the private's body, gathered the horse and Miss Wallace's saddlebag and taken them all to the funeral home before the sun came up this morning. I found Miss Wallace's horse grazing behind the funeral home this morning. It had a lady's saddle, it was not Army issue.

Nor did I need Tubby's magnifying glass to see the bits of Private Cochran's red hair and scalp lodged in the horse's front hooves. I also inspected the private's sidearm, which was inside the funeral home. The butt of his pistol was covered in dry blood, Miss Wallace's blood.

"Skinny had the saddlebag in his safe. I trust him, known him all my life, and everything that was in that saddlebag when that horse finished off Private Cochran was in that saddlebag when I opened it.

"There was the sapphire broach, beautiful and expensive; it probably belonged to Miss Wallace's mother. There was a piece of cloth pierced on the pin – the same fabric as her torn riding jacket. But sorry to say, major, there were also diamond bracelets, gold earrings, rubies and many exquisite pieces. But you'll never get to write those in your damnable ledger.

"In spite of Private Red's best efforts, Lily's horse and family heirlooms have been returned to Captain Wallace," I concluded. "They were returned to him by one of Key West's leading reverends and a group of citizens carrying food and the saddest news any father could bear. That good man is not alone today as he struggles to understand why his losses continue to mount, even with the war over."

The giant major stood and turned to allow the arresting officer to bind him in chains. Suddenly the major had a Bowie knife in his hand and let it fly at me.

I ducked, pulled my Colt and fired. I felt heat in my shoulder blade as the knife sunk in, slicing bone. The major fell, his forehead disfigured by the slug from my .45.

Actually, that part didn't happen. The major cooperated as he was restrained and walked away peacefully. But I did want to shoot him.

Colonel French got busy: "Provost marshal, please arrest the other two men mentioned in the ledger who boarded the *Savannah Wind*," he said. "And arrest anyone else whose names appear in this book."

The colonel thanked me quietly and we agreed that I would write up a report outlining the facts of the case, including witness testimony corroborating all that Tubs and I had learned. I suspect the best witness will be Captain Wallace himself, wronged, aggrieved and now out of family.

Speaking of which, I got Colonel French to agree to pay for expenses connected to the disposition of Lily Wallace's remains, Captain Wallace's harbor fees and other costs associated with the captain's time in Key West. The colonel agreed to all, including writing an official apology from the U.S. Army, Key West, to Captain Robert Wallace. I suspect the good captain will also hire an attorney and seek financial redress from the U.S. government.

After all, with the war lost, he is a restored citizen of the United States, with all the freedoms and benefits that entails.

10
Last Rites

Randy Becker

Every Memorial Day the little US flag placed on the grave by the Boy Scouts waves above the grave in Key West's cemetery, over in the corner near where one epitaph reads, "I told you I was sick." This grave however simply notes the resting place of one Sgt. Oren Peterson, 1892-1919.

Over the years wind, rain, hurricanes, and neglect have made the inscription nearly impossible to read. No one ever comes to place decorations on the grave. Sometime in the 1940s, a Royal Poinciana tree started itself aside the grave, gradually lending fiery majesty to the plot. It would be the tree's demise that would rattle a nearly 100-year-old cage of mystery and murder.

On September 17, 2017, a worker clearing Hurricane Irma debris in the cemetery uncovered the vault of Sgt. Peterson, now unearthed by the toppled tree's failed roots. The cover was askew, and the light of day penetrated for the first time since September 17, 1919, when the coffin had been lowered into the vault and the vault sealed. Taps had been played but there had been no family to receive the flag, just as there had been no family to receive the remains.

He was orphaned in a wreck on the reef off Key West, raised by the nuns at St. Mary's Star of the Sea. He would later say nothing about those years except that when he turned of age, he quickly left their tutelage and what he considered their abuse for the relatively easier discipline and respect of the US Army. On that day in 1910 when he left Key West, he vowed to the others standing at the bar that "someday, come hell or high water, I'll be back, and she'll be sorry." His life among the sisters had taught him fear and respect of authority so he thrived in the Army. By the time World War I had broken out, he had risen to the rank of Private First Class. He was in the first wave sent to the trenches, where he was also among the first wounded, receiving shrapnel wounds while wandering across a "no man's land." His "visit" to Europe was brief. Upon arrival back in the States for surgeries and recovery, he was sent to Fort Bragg, one of the first on that base. His recovery job, ironically, was as a mortician's helper, a job that became busier and busier as the pandemic flu moved throughout the land.

On that September day in 2017, Philip Allen, the cemetery worker looking into the depths of the disturbed vault became disturbed himself by what he saw. The ancient wood of an Army-issued simple coffin was rotted away leaving a visible corpse. But, instead of the mildewed and tattered Army uniform he expected on the body of the man identified on the tombstone, he was looking at the remnants of a nun's habit, a large metal cross still around the now-bony neck.

When Philip finally had composed himself, he went directly to the office of Cemetery Sexton, Russell Brittain, to report his find. Brittain informed the Key West Police that there was a mystery in the cemetery: his call was garbled, something about either having one body too many or one body missing. In the midst of post-Irma recovery, the call went to the bottom of the list, and stayed there when a brief follow-up indicated that the "body" in question was from 1919.

The work in the Army mortuary was acceptable to him because it provided him with special privileges (no one wanted to argue with or rebuke a member of the ghoul squad, as they were called). It also gave him a chance to get pocket-change by absorbing the pocket-change of the dead into his own pockets. A ring on a severed arm, a watch now and then, and some gold teeth all fell into his possession, like a modern-day Thénardier.

But, gnawing at him like a festering wound were his memories of his earlier years. The constant talk of sin, the sharp hit of the stick on his knuckles, the meager meals, the servitude which sapped his identity as a young man. Fellow mortuary workers knew him to be silent about his pre-Army life, but whenever asked about those years they would see him drink himself into a stupor. They assumed it was because of some kind of unspeakable loss ... only he knew it was because of some unspeakable hatred.

That hatred found a means of expression one morning when his manifest of the dead was faulty. He had one too many coffins, one too few bodies. Screw-ups like this were all-too-common, but the Army never wanted to know about them because it would mean someone higher up would need to be accountable. So, the lower levels learned to make work-arounds so the numbers came out even. Where the body of Sgt. Oren Peterson had gone to, he would never find out, nor would anyone else. All he knew there was this casket with its paperwork all complete, its destination Key West. It listed Sgt. Peterson a victim of the flu, with notations to mark the coffin sufficiently of this cause so people would avoid it even more so than a common coffin.

He had to work fast. Bodies were not allowed to remain long in their coffins awaiting transport. He had a coffin to modify and a telegram to send.

On that morning, one of the several coffins delivered to the station agent at Fayetteville, NC Atlantic Coast Line railroad station was one marked for immediate delivery to Key West on the morning's *Havana Special*. The paperwork and the coffin clearly showed "FLU" in big letters ... the coffin was handled gingerly by the assigned Negros, each of whom quickly when to the colored bathroom to wash up after loading the coffin on the baggage car of train 75.

The coffin gave off a strong odor of antiseptics, and that along with the large letters on it meant it was given a wide berth by the baggage car attendant. It was placed by itself at the far end of the baggage car, away from everything else, and the attendant had taken the extra precaution of spreading disinfecting power around it.

At about the same time, Sister Josephine Marie in Key West received a simple telegram: Greeting from the past -(stop)- hope you remember -(stop)- now successful businessman -(stop)- want to help convent - (stop)- Please meet me on Havana Special tomorrow out of Islamorada -(stop)- keep confidential -stop)- Bergland.

The Sister was acutely aware of the finances of the convent and knew that a gift, any gift of size, especially a gift of gratitude, would be of great assistance. Her vows of service required her to honor the request for confidentiality and so she burned the telegram and told none of the other Sisters about her planned trip north later that evening so she could be on the morning's southbound *Havana Special.* She was excited about the little trip, and the small amount of intrigue, and the promise of a gift whose donation through her would bring her a certain status among those who have chosen a life without status.

So it was that on the next morning two life paths were crossed by death. Bergland, now a deserter from the Army who had carefully concealed his departure with a death certificate in his name, would emerge from his specially prepared coffin which had been his home for over a day, into the relatively empty baggage car. He knew they were crossing the "Eighth Wonder of the World," the Seven Mile Bridge south of the Caribee Colony stop in Islamorada. The train had slowed to its crawl over the trestle and he knew from newspaper accounts that all eyes were on the sea around the train when it appeared the train was at sea. He stepped lightly out of his hiding place after ascertaining that the baggage man was nowhere to be seen. He softly closed the lid on the coffin, dusted himself off, and strode back into the passenger cars. It was in the first car, the one held for local traffic along the Special's long run (closest to the noise and filth of the locomotive) that he immediately saw her.

She sat alone and was the only person not looking out the windows. As always, she sat terribly erect, her eyes penetrating the air in search of some infraction of God's Holy Order. He could not detect even a glimmer of love, or compassion, or any Christ-like virtue in her gaze. When she saw him coming into the coach, it was as if a spirit of avarice came into her eyes, seeing him more as an object of possession than a person. He knew that gaze only too well. (Keep calm!)

Sister Josephine Marie arose from her seat, and greeted Bergland, "My, what a handsome man the sad little boy has become." (He hated her all the more.) "Sister," he began, "the years have been kind to you." (Lying is a sin, but not necessarily a mortal sin, he recalled as his knuckles ached their memories.)

"What I have to tell you is so blessed and wonderful. But it involves some investments here in the Keys, so I would rather tell you about it in a more secluded place where we might have privacy, like the sanctity of a confessional."

"My son (O, damn you, I am not your son)," the Sister responded, "where then?"

"Follow me." And with that he headed back into the baggage car. It was still deserted and at its end the coffin stood by itself.

He led the Sister to the coffin and quietly said "First, a quick prayer for this poor departed soldier, if you please." As the Sister lowered her head she felt the cord around her neck, the cord of her crucifix, tightening so suddenly that all she could do was think "O, my God, forgive him for he knows not ..." before losing consciousness.

Bergland opened the coffin and dropped the nun into the empty space. He straightened her habit (can't be holy when you are messy!) and replaced her crucifix onto her bosom. Then he closed and sealed the lid of the coffin. "Bless you, for you have sinned," was his benediction over the coffin. He quickly strode into the coach, grabbed the nun's seat check from above where she had been seated so everyone would be accounted for, and kept walking back toward the dining car. There was still time for a late breakfast as the train eased into Craig.

The more than twenty minutes between Islamorada and Craig was the longest spell between stations on the Overseas Railroad, and the baggage man had used the time, as he did every trip, to enjoy his own breakfast. Upon returning to the baggage car he was surprised to see what looked like a shoe print in the disinfecting powder around the coffin.

This gave the superstitious man a start ... had the corpse risen from the dead? He tentatively tried to lift the coffin, but it was weighty beyond his single efforts. No, the body was still there. Maybe he had stepped in the powder as he had spread it. Or one of the head-end men overnight had stepped into it. With a sigh of relief he went back to his desk and sorted the items to be off-loaded at upcoming stations.

When the train pulled into the station on Trumbo Point in Key West, the undertaker's wagon was waiting for its load. He whistled to several of the black men waiting around the station to come and unload the gruesome cargo. While they were doing that duty, he chatted with the undertaker, who kept his own distance from the flu-labeled coffin. A grave had already been prepared for a quick disposal of this unwanted, diseased intrusion from the mainland. The military marker had been ordered. No family left in town. Military honors would be at 2pm, and it would all be sealed up by 2:30pm. He had masons standing by to make sure the flu was not going to spread.

While that conversation was taking place, a well-composed Bergland strolled across the tracks to the waiting Peninsular & Occidental Steamship Company steamer for Havana. At 12:20pm, with a long whistle the steamer set out, with the manifest showing tickets, among others, for Bergland and a Josephine Marie of the Convent of St. Mary Star of the Sea. Bergland stopped a young woman passing by and said, "I think that lovely nun who was sitting here dropped her ticket .... Will you please take it up to the Bursar. Thank you."

In the Convent, Mother Superior was upset when, at dinner that night, Sister Josephine Marie was absent. She had not been given leave and an examination of the Sister's cell seemed to indicate that she had not slept there the night before. Consternation turned to anger to worry as the hours passed. Finally, a note was delivered to Convent. It had been found on the steamship pier, on a bench for departing passengers. The agent delivering it was apologetic but said they were short-handed what with the war on and all.

The note was brief: Found a love greater than Christ. Will follow him to the end of the earth. (Sister Josephine) Marie.

It was in the lovely Palmer Method handwriting of the Sister, just as she had taught all her students over the years. Over and over again, insistently until they got it right, so they could write just as beautifully as she could. Enforced by slaps to the back of the head, reinforced with time in the corner, demanded by that long wooden ruler. No doubt, it was her handwriting.

To protect the sanctity of the Convent, and with this proof of immorality and deceit in hand, the Mother Superior filed no report with the police. She made only the simplest of notations in the books of the Convent: "departed."

By the time the Police had dealt with many more serious repercussions of Hurricane Irma, a detective made another visit to the cemetery. Yes, it was a nun where a soldier should be. No doubt about that. Army records showed a Sgt. Peterson had been sent home to Key West for burial in 1919. They also showed that about the same time no one had deserted from Ft. Bragg, and many had died from the flu. In fact the epidemic had become so bad about a dozen other lost souls, with no next-of-kin, had been buried in a common grave on the fort, its exact location now lost to history. If you were to read the records, a PFC Bergland would be on the list. "Those were terrible times, with more dying from the flu than from the war," the agent at the Army records office added.

So, who was this nun? No nun had been reported missing, and no one else was reported missing about the time of the burial. Everyone was accounted for, except Sgt. Oren Peterson. To the Army he is buried in Key West, except he isn't. But the Army never makes mistakes.

In the tradition which had surrounded these circumstances since their beginning, the official decision by present-day law enforcement (Police and State's Attorney) was to repair the grave and reseal it as it has been before Hurricane Irma, ready for a new flag next Memorial Day. And to be safe, make sure no new trees grow near it.

But, I am told, just to be safe, the cemetery workers had a priest from St. Marys come by and blessed the re-interment after the repairs, but without mentioning what they knew was inside.

Maybe the next time you walk the cemetery you will offer your own last rites for Sgt. Peterson, or Sister Josephine Marie, or for whoever is also out there.

About The Authors

1

Jack Mazur

Jack Mazur studied creative writing at Southern Connecticut State University in the 1980s under Richard Russo, who would go on to win the Pulitzer for *Empire Falls* in 2005 or so.

2

Shirrel Rhoades

Shirrel Rhoades is a writer, critic, filmmaker, former college professor, art collector, museum president, and publisher. These days, he calls Key West home. He is the author of *Four Fingers Four Minute Mysteries, The Devil's Hop Yard,* and *Front Row at the Movies,* among many other titles. He and his wife share their historic classic temple revival style house in Old Town with a dog and ½ cat, a few boarders, and a number of stray iguanas.

3

Rick Ollerman

Rick Ollerman is the author of four novels ***TURNABOUT, SHALLOW SECRETS, TRUTH ALWAYS KILLS, MAD DOG BARKED,*** and one non-fiction collection: ***HARDBOILED, NOIR AND GOLD MEDALS: ESSAYS ON CRIME FICTION WRITERS FROM THE '50S THROUGH THE '90S***. He also edited and contributed to ***PAPERBACK CONFIDENTIAL***, a book containing 132 short bios about writers from the paperback original era through the present . He also edits the crime fiction magazine **DOWN & OUT: THE MAGAZINE**, and two anthologies are scheduled for

2018. His fifth novel, **NO BAD DAYS**, will be released in 2018 as a sequel to his last two books.

4

Albert L. Kelley

Albert L. Kelley is an attorney located in Key West, Florida and concentrates primarily in the areas of business, corporations, contracts, copyright, trademark, and entertainment law.

In 2002, Al Kelley planned, developed and produced an award -winning video biography of Capt. Tony Tarracino, internationally known saloon owner, gambler, charter boat captain, gunrunner and Mayor of Key West (Tarracino was the subject of Jimmy Buffett's song "Last Mango In Paris").

Aside from his numerous newspaper columns, Al Kelley has written books, screenplays, poetry and short stories.

5

Justin Maxwell
(a/k/a Wayne "Skip" Kadar)

Justin Maxwell is the pen name of Wayne "Skip" Kadar. He taught at the high school level for several years then became a high school principal. After 16 years as a principal he retired from education. In retirement he worked as a harbor master at a marina on the Great Lakes and researched and wrote eight historically factual books about the Great Lakes region; books about ships that now lie on the bottom of the freshwater seas.

6

Barthélemy Banks

Barthélemy Banks is the *nom de plume* of a former supervisor for a publishing company that was secretly backed by the CIA. He spent a number of years in the Bahamas where he rubbed elbows with spies, smugglers, international bankers, and reclusive millionaires. Today, he lives on a remote island, where he finds it safe to write about the clandestine world he knows so well.

7

R. K. Simpson

R.K. Simpson lives in Alexandria, Virginia, with his wife Patty. He is a graduate of Dartmouth College and a veteran of the Marine Corps and the war in Vietnam. He served as a diplomat in several of our embassies in Europe and Africa for over twenty years. Upon retiring from the government, he worked as a pediatric nurse for fifteen years. He has three adult children.

8

Robert Coburn

Robert Coburn is originally from Norfolk, Virginia. After high school in Norfolk, he spent three years in the US Army as a helicopter crew chief stationed in Berlin, Germany. He returned home to attend college at Richmond Professional Institute (Now VCU) in Richmond, Virginia, where he earned a Bachelor of Science degree in Advertising. He also met his wife in Richmond while a student there.

Coburn has worked at major advertising agencies in New York and Los Angeles. His ads have won top awards both nationally and internationally. He is an instrument rated commercial pilot and plays saxophone. He and his wife now live in Carmel, California.

9

John Guerra

John Guerra is a career reporter and writer. As a former editor and reporter at Key West's daily newspaper, he has witnessed and written about the daily turn of events as well as witnessed some of the biggest events in the island's history. He has written for newspapers, magazines and websites around the country and has written dozens of short stories. Born in Washington, D.C., he graduated from the University of Maryland with a degree in journalism and Latin American history. *Maddie's Gone* and *Just Us* are his first two novels. He has two other books in the works.

10

Randy Becker

Randolph W.B. Becker is an inveterate traveler who always seeks to be more a temporary resident than a tourist. You will most often find him on public transit, eating at neighborhood restaurants, finding what you do when you get lost, and braving barely-known languages to converse with newly found friends over a glass of red wine. When not on the move, he lives in Key West, Conch Republic.

ABSOLUTELY AMAZING eBOOKS

AbsolutelyAmazingEbooks.com
or AA-eBooks.com

www.ingramcontent.com/pod-product-compliance
Lightning Source LLC
Chambersburg PA
CBHW050406030726
47503CB00006B/2044